Jake limped o W9-AVG-029 *pushed it gently open, then stood transfixed*

Chaos. Complete, utter chaos.

Two children were sitting on the floor by the fire, carefully tying berries to some rather battered branches that looked as if they had come off the conifer hedge at the back of the country club. But it was the woman who held his attention.

Tall, slender, with rather wild fair hair escaping from a ponytail and jeans that had definitely seen better days, she was twisting another of the branches into the heavy iron hoop over the refectory table, festooning the light with a makeshift attempt at a Christmas decoration that did nothing to improve it.

He'd never seen her before. He would have recognized her, he was sure, if he had. So who the—

The woman turned and her eyes flew wide. "Oh—"

Dropping down, she slid off the edge of the table and came toward him with a haphazard attempt at a smile. "Um—I imagine you're Jake Forrester?" she asked, her voice a little uneven, and he hardened himself against her undoubted appeal and her desperate eyes.

Dear Reader,

Isn't it amazing how quickly Christmas comes round? How wonderfully, reliably, *relentlessly* often? And it's so expensive, too. Expectations are unrealistically high, emotions are near the surface and there's nothing quite like it for underlining not only the joys but the tragedies and disappointments of our lives, too.

So imagine you've suddenly been made homeless and your life is in total chaos. Or that Christmas is the worst time in the world for you and the only way you can deal with it is to pretend it doesn't happen. Then imagine what happens when these two people are thrown together at Christmastime—and put three children and a dog into the mix. Stir well and make a wish….

I cried buckets writing this, so a word of warning—if you're a softy, put on your waterproof mascara! And I hope you have a wonderful Christmas.

With love,

Caroline

CAROLINE ANDERSON
Their Christmas Family Miracle

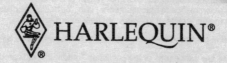

HARLEQUIN®

TORONTO • NEW YORK • LONDON
AMSTERDAM • PARIS • SYDNEY • HAMBURG
STOCKHOLM • ATHENS • TOKYO • MILAN • MADRID
PRAGUE • WARSAW • BUDAPEST • AUCKLAND

Recycling programs
for this product may
not exist in your area.

ISBN-13: 978-0-373-17629-8

THEIR CHRISTMAS FAMILY MIRACLE

First North American Publication 2009.

www.eHarlequin.com

Printed in U.S.A.

Caroline Anderson has the mind of a butterfly. She's been a nurse, a secretary, a teacher, run her own soft-furnishing business and now she's settled on writing. She says, "I was looking for that elusive something. I finally realized it was variety, and now I have it in abundance. Every book brings new horizons and new friends, and in between books I have learned to be a juggler. My teacher husband, John, and I have two beautiful and talented daughters, Sarah and Hannah, umpteen pets and several acres of Suffolk that nature tries to reclaim every time we turn our backs!"

CHAPTER ONE

'WE NEED to talk.'

Amelia sat back on her heels and looked up at her sister with a sinking heart. She'd heard them arguing, heard her brother-in-law's harsh, bitter tone, heard the slamming of the doors, then her sister's approaching footsteps on the stairs. And she knew what was coming.

What she didn't know was how to deal with it.

'This isn't working,' she said calmly.

'No.' Laura looked awkward and acutely uncomfortable, but she also looked a little relieved that Amelia had made it easy for her. Again. Her hands clenched and unclenched nervously. 'It's not me—it's Andy. Well, and me, really, I suppose. It's the kids. They just—run around all the time, and the baby cries all night, and Andy's tired. He's supposed to be having a rest over Christmas, and instead—it's not their fault, Millie, but having the children here is difficult, we're just not used to it. And the dog, really, is the last straw. So—yes, I'm sorry, but—if you could find somewhere as soon as possible after Christmas—'

Amelia set aside the washing she was folding and got up, shaking her head, the thought of staying where she—

no, where her *children* were not wanted, anathema to her.
'It's OK. Don't apologise. It's a terrible imposition. Don't
worry about it, we'll go now. I'll just pack their things and
we'll get out of your hair—'

'I thought you didn't have anywhere to go?'

She didn't. Or money to pay for it, but that was hardly
her sister's fault, was it? 'Don't worry,' she said again.
'We'll go to Kate's.'

But crossing her fingers behind her back was pointless.
Kate lived in a tiny cottage, one up one down, with hardly
room for her and her own daughter. There was no way the
four of them and the dog could squeeze in, too. But her
sister didn't know that, and her shoulders dropped in relief.

'I'll help you get their things together,' she said quickly,
and disappeared, presumably to comb the house for any
trace of their presence while Amelia sagged against the
wall, shutting her eyes hard against the bitter sting of tears
and fighting down the sob of desperation that was rising in
her throat. Two and a half days to Christmas.

Short, dark, chaotic days in which she had no hope of
finding anywhere for them to go or another job to pay for
it. And, just to make it worse, they were in the grip of an
unseasonably cold snap, so even if they were driven to it,
there was no way they could sleep in the car. Not without
running the engine, and that wasn't an option, since she
probably only had just enough fuel to get away from her
sister's house with her pride intact.

And, as it was the only thing she had left, that was a
priority.

Sucking in a good, deep breath, she gathered up the
baby's clothes and started packing them haphazardly, then

stopped herself. She had to prioritise. Things for the next twenty-four hours in one little bag, then everything else she could sort out later once they'd arrived at wherever they were going. She sorted, shuffled, packed the baby's clothes, then her own, then finally went into the bedroom Kitty and Edward were sharing and packed their clothes and toys, with her mind firmly shut down and her thoughts banished for now.

She could think later. There'd be time to think once they were out of here. In the meantime, she needed to gather up the children and any other bits and pieces she'd overlooked and get them out before she totally lost it. She went down with the bags hanging like bunches of grapes from her fingers, dumped them in the hall and went into the euphemistically entitled family room, where her children were lying on their tummies watching the TV with the dog between them.

Not on the sofa again, mercifully.

'Kitty? Edward? Come and help me look for all your things, because we're going to go and see Kate and Megan.'

'What—now?' Edward asked, twisting round, his face sceptical. 'It's nearly lunch time.'

'Are we going to Kate's for lunch?' Kitty asked brightly.

'Yes. It's a surprise.' A surprise for Kate, at least, she thought, hustling them through the house and gathering up the last few traces of their brief but eventful stay.

'Why do we need all our things to go and see Kate and Megan for lunch?' Kitty asked, but Edward got there first and shushed her. Bless his heart. Eight years old and she'd be lost without him.

They met up with Laura in the kitchen, her face strained, a bag in her hand.

'I found these,' she said, giving it to Amelia. 'The baby's bottles. There was one in the dishwasher, too.'

'Thanks. Right, well, I just need to get the baby up and fold his cot, and we'll be out of your hair.'

She retreated upstairs to get him. Poor Thomas. He whimpered and snuggled into her as she picked him up, and she collapsed his travel cot one-handed and bumped it down the stairs. Their stuff was piled by the door, and she wondered if Andy might come out of his study and give them a hand to load it into her car, but the door stayed resolutely shut throughout.

It was just as well. It would save her the bother of being civil.

She put the baby in his seat, the cold air bringing him wide awake and protesting, threw their things into the boot and buckled the other two in, with Rufus on the floor in the front, before turning to her sister with her last remnant of pride and meeting her eyes.

'Thank you for having us. I'm sorry it was so difficult.'

Laura's face creased in a mixture of distress and embarrassment. 'Oh, don't. I'm so sorry, Millie. I hope you get sorted out. Here, these are for the children.' She handed over a bag of presents, all beautifully wrapped. Of course. They would be. Also expensive and impossible to compete with. And that wasn't what it was supposed to be about, but she took them, her arm working on autopilot.

'Thank you. I'm afraid I haven't got round to getting yours yet—'

'It doesn't matter. I hope you find somewhere nice soon. And—take this, please. I know money's tight for you at the moment, but it might give you the first month's rent or deposit—'

She stared at the cheque. 'Laura, I can't—'

'Yes, you can. Please. Owe me, if you have to, but take it. It's the least I can do.'

So she took it, stuffing it into her pocket without looking at it. 'I'll pay you back as soon as I can.'

'Whenever. Have a good Christmas.'

How she found that smile she'd never know. 'And you,' she said, unable to bring herself to say the actual words, and getting behind the wheel and dropping the presents into the passenger footwell next to Rufus, she shut the door before her sister could lean in and hug her, started the engine and drove away.

'Mummy, why *are* we taking all our Christmas presents and Rufus and the cot and everything to Kate and Megan's for lunch?' Kitty asked, still obviously troubled and confused, as well she might be.

Damn Laura. Damn Andy. And especially damn David. She schooled her expression and threw a smile over her shoulder at her little daughter. 'Well, we aren't going to stay with Auntie Laura and Uncle Andy any more, so after we've had lunch we're going to go somewhere else to stay,' she said.

'Why? Don't they like us?'

Ouch. 'Of course they do,' she lied, 'but they just need a bit of space.'

'So where *are* we going?'

It was a very good question, but one Millie didn't have a hope of answering right now…

* * *

It was an ominous sound.

He'd heard it before, knew instantly what it was, and Jake felt his mouth dry and his heart begin to pound. He glanced up over his shoulder, swore softly and turned, skiing sideways straight across and down the mountain, pushing off on his sticks and plunging down and away from the path of the avalanche that was threatening to wipe him out, his legs driving him forward out of its reach.

The choking powder cloud it threw up engulfed him, blinding him as the raging, roaring monster shot past behind him. The snow was shaking under his skis, the air almost solid with the fine snow thrown up as the snowfield covering the side of the ridge collapsed and thundered down towards the valley floor below.

He was skiing blind, praying that he was still heading in the right direction, hoping that the little stand of trees down to his left was now above him and not still in front of him, because at the speed he was travelling to hit one could be fatal.

It wasn't fatal, he discovered. It was just unbelievably, immensely painful. He bounced off a tree, then felt himself lifted up and carried on by the snow—down towards the scattered tumble of rocks at the bottom of the snowfield.

Hell.

With his last vestige of self-preservation, he triggered the airbags of his avalanche pack, and then he hit the rocks...

'Can you squeeze in a few more for lunch?'

Kate took one look at them all, opened the door wide

and ushered them inside. 'What on earth is going on?' she asked, her concerned eyes seeking out the truth from Millie's face.

'We've come for lunch,' Kitty said, still sounding puzzled. 'And then we're going to find somewhere to live. Auntie Laura and Uncle Andy don't want us. Mummy says they need space, but I don't think they like us.'

'Of course they do, darling. They're just very busy, that's all.'

Kate's eyes flicked down to Kitty with the dog at her side, to Edward, standing silently and saying nothing, and back to Millie. 'Nice timing,' she said flatly, reading between the lines.

'Tell me about it,' she muttered. 'Got any good ideas?'

Kate laughed slightly hysterically and handed the three older children a bag of chocolate coins off the tree. 'Here, guys, go and get stuck into these while Mummy and I have a chat. Megan, share nicely and don't give any chocolate to Rufus.'

'I *always* share nicely! Come on, we can share them out—and Rufus, you're not having *any*!'

Rolling her eyes, Kate towed Amelia down to the other end of the narrow room that was the entire living space in her little cottage, put the kettle on and raised an eyebrow. 'Well?'

She shifted Thomas into a more comfortable position in her arms. 'They aren't really child-orientated. They don't have any, and I'm not sure if it's because they haven't got round to it or because they really don't like them,' Millie said softly.

'And your lot were too much of a dose of reality?'

She smiled a little tightly. 'The dog got on the sofa, and Thomas is teething.'

'Ah.' Kate looked down at the tired, grizzling baby in his mother's arms and her kind face crumpled. 'Oh, Amelia, I'm so sorry,' she murmured under her breath. 'I can't believe they kicked you out just before Christmas!'

'They didn't. They wanted me to look for somewhere afterwards, but…'

'But—?'

She shrugged. 'My pride got in the way,' she said, hating the little catch in her voice. 'And now my kids have nowhere to go for Christmas. And convincing a landlord to give me a house before I can get another job is going to be tricky, and that's not going to happen any time soon if the response to my CV continues to be as resoundingly successful as it's being at the moment, and anyway the letting agents aren't going to be able to find us anything this close to Christmas. I could *kill* David for cutting off the maintenance,' she added under her breath, a little catch in her voice.

'Go ahead—I'll be a character witness for you in court,' Kate growled, then she leant back, folded her arms and chewed her lip thoughtfully. 'I wonder…?'

'What?'

'You could have Jake's house,' she said softly. 'My boss. I would say stay here, but I've got my parents and my sister coming for Christmas Day and I can hardly fit us all in as it is, but there's tons of room at Jake's. He's away until the middle of January. He always goes away at Christmas for a month—he shuts the office, gives everyone three weeks off on full pay and leaves the country before the office party, and I have the keys to keep an eye on it. And it's just sitting there, the most fabulous house, and it's just made for Christmas.'

'Won't he mind?'

'What, Jake? No. He wouldn't give a damn. You won't do it any harm, after all, will you? It's hundreds of years old and it's survived. What harm can you do it?'

What harm? She felt rising panic just thinking about it. 'I couldn't—'

'Don't be daft. Where else are you going to go? Besides, with the weather so cold it'll be much better for the house to have the heating on full and the fire lit. He'll be grateful when he finds out, and besides, Jake's generous to a fault. He'd want you to have it. Truly.'

Amelia hesitated. Kate seemed so convinced he wouldn't mind. 'You'd better ring him, then,' she said in the end. 'But tell him I'll give him money for rent just as soon as I can—'

Kate shook her head. 'No. I can't. I don't have the number, but I know he'd say yes,' she said, and Amelia's heart sank.

'Well, then, we can't stay there. Not without asking—'

'Millie, really. It'll be all right. He'd die before he'd let you be homeless over Christmas and there's no way he'd take money off you. Believe me, he'd want you to have the house.'

Still she hesitated, searching Kate's face for any sign of uncertainty, but if she felt any, Kate was keeping it to herself, and besides, Amelia was so out of options she couldn't afford the luxury of scruples, and in the end she gave in.

'Are you sure?'

'Absolutely. There won't be any food there, his house-keeper will have emptied the fridge, but I've got some basics I can let you have and bread and stuff, and there's bound to be something in the freezer and the cupboards to tide you over until you can replace it. We'll go over there the minute we've had lunch and settle you in. It'll be great—fantastic! You'll love it.'

'Love what?' Kitty asked, sidling up with chocolate all round her mouth and a doubtful expression on her face.

'My boss's house. He's gone away, and he's going to let you borrow it.'

'Let?' Millie said softly under her breath, but Kate just flashed her a smile and shrugged.

'Well, he would if he knew... OK, lunch first, and then let's go!'

It was, as Kate had said, the most fabulous house.

A beautiful old Tudor manor house, it had been in its time a farm and then a small hotel and country club, she explained, and then Jake had bought it and moved his offices out here into the Berkshire countryside. He lived in the house, and there was an office suite housing Jake's centre of operations in the former country club buildings on the far side of the old walled kitchen garden. There was a swimming pool, a sauna and steam room and a squash court over there, Kate told her as they pulled up outside on the broad gravel sweep, and all the facilities were available to the staff and their families.

Further evidence of his apparent generosity.

But it was the house which drew Amelia—old mellow

red brick, with a beautiful Dutch gabled porch set in the centre, and as Kate opened the huge, heavy oak door that bore the scars of countless generations and ushered them into the great entrance hall, even the children fell silent.

'Wow,' Edward said after a long, breathless moment.

Wow, indeed. Amelia stared around her, dumbstruck. There was a beautiful, ancient oak staircase on her left, and across the wide hall which ran from side to side were several lovely old doors which must lead to the principal rooms.

She ran her hand over the top of the newel post, once heavily carved, the carving now almost worn away by the passage of generations of hands. She could feel them all, stretching back four hundred years, the young, the old, the children who'd been born and grown old and died here, sheltered and protected by this beautiful, magnificent old house, and ridiculous though it was, as the front door closed behind them, she felt as if the house was gathering them up into its heart.

'Come on, I'll give you a quick tour,' Kate said, going down the corridor to the left, and they all trooped after her, the children still in a state of awe. The carpet under her feet must be a good inch thick, she thought numbly. Just how rich *was* this guy?

As Kate opened the door in front of her and they went into a vast and beautifully furnished sitting room with a huge bay window at the side overlooking what must surely be acres of parkland, she got her answer, and she felt her jaw drop.

Very rich. Fabulously, spectacularly rich, without a shadow of a doubt.

And yet he was gone, abandoning this beautiful house in which he lived alone to spend Christmas on a ski slope.

She felt tears prick her eyes, strangely sorry for a man she'd never met, who'd furnished his house with such love and attention to detail, and yet didn't apparently want to stay in it at the time of year when it must surely be at its most welcoming.

'Why?' she asked, turning to Kate in confusion. 'Why does he go?'

Kate shrugged. 'Nobody really knows. Or nobody talks about it. There aren't very many people who've worked for him that long. I've been his PA for a little over three years, since he moved the business here from London, and he doesn't talk about himself.'

'How sad.'

'Sad? No. Not Jake. He's not sad. He's crazy, he has some pretty wacky ideas and they nearly always work, and he's an amazingly thoughtful boss, but he's intensely private. Nobody knows anything about him, really, although he always makes a point of asking about Megan, for instance. But I don't think he's sad. I think he's just a loner and he likes to ski. Come and see the rest.'

They went back down the hall, along the squishy pile carpet that absorbed all the sound of their feet, past all the lovely old doors while Kate opened them one by one and showed them the rooms in turn.

A dining room with a huge table and oak-panelled walls; another sitting room, much smaller than the first, with a plasma TV in the corner, book-lined walls, battered leather sofas and all the evidence that this was his very personal retreat. There was a study at the front of the house which they didn't enter; and then finally the room Kate called the breakfast room—huge again, but with the same informality as the little sitting room, with foot-wide oak boards on the floor and a great big old refectory table covered in the scars of generations and just made for family living.

And the kitchen off it was, as she might have expected, also designed for a family—or entertaining on an epic scale. Vast, with duck-egg blue painted cabinets under thick, oiled wood worktops, a gleaming white four-oven Aga in the inglenook, and in the middle a granite-topped island with stools pulled up to it. It was a kitchen to die for, the kitchen of her dreams and fantasies, and it took her breath away. It took all their breaths away.

The children stared round it in stunned silence, Edward motionless, Kitty running her fingers reverently over the highly polished black granite, lingering over the tiny gold sparkles trapped deep inside the stone. Edward was the first to recover.

'Are we really going to stay here?' he asked, finally finding his voice, and she shook her head in disbelief.

'I don't think so.'

'Of course you are!'

'Kate, we can't—'

'Rubbish! Of course you can. It's only for a week or two. Come and see the bedrooms.'

Amelia shifted Thomas to her other hip and followed Kate up the gently creaking stairs, the children trailing awestruck in her wake, listening to Megan chattering about when they'd stayed there earlier in the year.

'That's Jake's room,' Kate said, turning away from it,

and Amelia felt a prickle of curiosity. What would his room be like? Opulent? Austere? Monastic?

No, not monastic. This man was a sensualist, she realised, fingering the curtains in the bedroom Kate led them into. Pure silk, lined with padding for warmth and that feeling of luxury that pervaded the entire house. Definitely not monastic.

'All the rooms are like this—except for some in the attic, which are a bit simpler,' Kate told her. 'You could take your pick but I'd have the ones upstairs. They're nicer.'

'How many are there?' she asked, amazed.

'Ten. Seven en suite, five on this floor and two above, and three more in the attic which share a bathroom. Those are the simpler ones. He entertains business clients here quite often, and they love it. So many people have offered to buy it, but he just laughs and says no.'

'I should think so. Oh, Kate—what if we ruin something?'

'You won't ruin it. The last person to stay here knocked a pot of coffee over on the bedroom carpet. He just had it cleaned.'

Millie didn't bother to point out that the last person to stay here had been invited—not to mention an adult who presumably was either a friend or of some commercial interest to their unknowing host.

'Can we see the attic? The simple rooms? It sounds more like our thing.'

'Sure. Megan, why don't you show Kitty and Edward your favourite room?'

The children ran upstairs after Megan, freed from their trance now and getting excited as the reality of it began to sink in, and she turned to Kate and took her arm. 'Kate, we can't possibly stay here without asking him,' she said urgently, her voice low. 'It would be so rude—and I just know something'll get damaged.'

'Don't be silly. Come on, I'll show you *my* favourite room. It's lovely, you'll adore it. Megan and I stayed here when my pipes froze last February, and it was bliss. It's got a gorgeous bed.'

'They've all got gorgeous beds.'

They had. Four-posters, with great heavy carved posts and silk canopies, or half testers with just the head end of the bed clothed in sumptuous drapes.

Except for the three Kate showed her now. In the first one, instead of a four-poster there was a great big old brass and iron bedstead, the whole style of the room much simpler and somehow less terrifying, even though the quality of the furnishings was every bit as good, and in the adjoining room was an antique child-sized sleigh bed that looked safe and inviting.

It was clearly intended to be a nursery, and would be perfect for Thomas, she thought wistfully, and beside it was a twin room with two black iron beds, again decorated more simply, and Megan and Kitty were sitting on the beds and bouncing, while giggles rose from their throats and Edward pretended to be too old for such nonsense and looked on longingly.

'We could sleep up here,' she agreed at last. 'And we could spend the days in the breakfast room.' Even the children couldn't hurt that old table...

'There's a playroom—come and see,' Megan said, pelting out of the room with the other children in hot pursuit, and Amelia followed them to where the landing widened and there were big sofas and another TV and lots and lots of books and toys.

'He said he had this area done for people who came with children, so they'd have somewhere to go where they could let their hair down a bit,' Kate explained, and then smiled. 'You see—he doesn't mind children being in the house. If he did, why would he have done this?'

Why, indeed? There was even a stair gate, she noticed, made of oak and folded back against the banisters. And somehow she didn't mind the idea of tucking them away in what amounted to the servants' quarters nearly as much.

'I'll help you bring everything up,' Kate said. 'Kids, come and help. You can carry some of your stuff.'

It only took one journey because most of their possessions were in storage, packed away in a unit on the edge of town, waiting for the time when she could find a way to house them in a place of their own again. Hopefully, this time with a landlord who wouldn't take the first opportunity to get them out.

And then, with everything installed, she let Rufus out of the car and took him for a little run on the grass at the side of the drive. Poor little dog. He was so confused but, so long as he was with her and the children, he was as good as gold, and she felt her eyes fill with tears.

If David had had his way, the dog would have been put down because of his health problems, but she'd struggled to keep up the insurance premiums to maintain his veterinary cover, knowing that the moment they lapsed, her funding for the dog's health and well-being would come to a grinding halt.

And that would be the end of Rufus.

She couldn't allow that to happen. The little Cavalier King Charles spaniel that she'd rescued as a puppy had been a lifeline for the children in the last few dreadful years, and she owed him more than she could ever say. So his premiums were paid, even if it meant she couldn't eat.

'Mummy, it's lovely here,' Kitty said, coming up to her and snuggling her tiny, chilly hand into Millie's. 'Can we stay for ever?'

Oh, I wish, she thought, but she ruffled Kitty's hair and smiled. 'No, darling—but we can stay until after Christmas, and then we'll find another house.'

'Promise?'

She crossed her fingers behind her back. 'Promise,' she said, and hoped that fate wouldn't make her a liar.

He couldn't breathe.

For a moment he thought he was buried despite his avalanche pack, and for that fleeting moment in time he felt fear swamp him, but then he realised he was lying face down in the snow.

His legs were buried in the solidified aftermath of the avalanche, but near the surface, and his body was mostly on the top. He tipped his head awkwardly, and a searing pain shot through his shoulder and down his left arm. Damn. He tried again, more cautiously this time, and the snow on his goggles slid off, showering his face with ice crystals that stung his skin in the cold, sharp air. He breathed deeply and opened his eyes and saw daylight. The last traces of it, the shadows long as night approached.

He managed to clear the snow from around his arms, and

shook his head to clear his goggles better and regretted it instantly. He gave the pain a moment, and then began to yell into the silence of the fading light.

He yelled for what seemed like hours, and then, like a miracle, he heard voices.

'Help!' he bellowed again, and waved, blanking out the pain.

And help came, in the form of big, burly lads who broke away the snow surrounding him, dug his legs out and helped him struggle free. Dear God, he hurt. Everywhere, but most particularly his left arm and his left knee, he realised. Where he'd hit the tree. Or the rocks. No, he'd hurt them on the tree, he remembered, but the rocks certainly hadn't helped and he was going to have a million bruises.

'Can you ski back down?' they asked, and he realised he was still wearing his skis. The bindings had held, even through that. He got up and tested his left leg and winced, but it was holding his weight, and the right one was fine. He nodded and, cradling his left arm against his chest, he picked his way off the rock field to the edge, then followed them slowly down the mountain to the village.

He was shipped off to hospital the moment they arrived back, and he was prodded and poked and tutted over for what seemed like an age. And then, finally, they put his arm in a temporary cast, gave him a nice fat shot of something blissful and he escaped into the blessed oblivion of sleep...

CHAPTER TWO

SHE refused to let Kate turn up the heating.

'We'll be fine,' she protested. 'Believe me, this isn't cold.'

'It's only on frost protection!'

'It's fine. We're used to it. Please, I really don't want to argue about this. We have jumpers.'

'Well, at least light the woodburner,' Kate said, relenting with a sigh. 'There's a huge stack of logs outside the back door.'

'I can't use his logs! Logs are expensive!'

Kate just laughed. 'Not if you own several acres of woodland. He has more logs than he knows what to do with. We all use them. I throw some into the boot of my car every day and take them home to burn overnight, and so does everyone else. Really, you can't let the kids be cold, Millie. Just use the wood.'

So she did. She lit the fire, stood the heavy black mesh guard in front of it and the children settled down on the rug with Rufus and watched the television while she made them something quick and simple for supper. Even Thomas was good, managing to eat his supper without spitting it out all over the room or screaming the place down, and Amelia felt herself start to relax.

And when the wind picked up in the night and the old house creaked and groaned, it was just as if it was settling down, turning up its collar against the wind and wrapping its arms around them all to keep them warm.

Fanciful nonsense.

But it felt real, and when she got up in the morning and tiptoed downstairs to check the fire before the children woke, she found Rufus fast asleep on the rug in front of the woodburner, and he lifted his head and wagged his tail. She picked him up and hugged him, tears of relief prickling her eyes because finally, for the first time in months, she felt—even if it would only be for a few days—as if they were safe.

She filled up the fire, amazed that it had stayed alight, and made herself a cup of tea while Rufus went out in the garden for a moment. Then she took advantage of the quiet time and sat with him by the fire to drink her tea and contemplate her next move.

Rattling the cage of the job agencies, of course. What choice was there? Without a job, she couldn't hope to get a house. And she needed to get some food in. Maybe a small chicken? She could roast it, and put a few sausages round it, and it would be much cheaper than a turkey. Just as well, as she was trying to stretch the small amount of money she had left for as long as possible.

She thought of the extravagant Christmases she'd had with David in the past, the lavish presents, the wasted food, and wondered if the children felt cheated. Probably, but Christmas was just one of the many ways in which he'd let them down on a regular basis, so she was sure they'd just take it all in their stride.

Unlike being homeless, she thought, getting to her feet and washing out her mug before going upstairs to start the day. They were finding that really difficult and confusing, and all the chopping and changing was making them feel insecure. And she hated that. But there was Laura's cheque, which meant she might be able to find somewhere sooner—even if she would have to pay her back, just for the sake of her pride.

So, bearing the cheque in mind, she spent part of the morning on the phone trying to find somewhere to live, but the next day would be Christmas Eve and realistically nobody wanted to show her anything until after the Christmas period was over, and the job agencies were no more helpful. Nobody, apparently, was looking for a translator at the moment, so abandoning her search until after Christmas, she took the kids out for a long walk around the grounds, with Thomas in his stroller and Rufus sniffing the ground and having a wonderful time while Kitty and Edward ran around shrieking and giggling.

And there was nobody to hear, nobody to complain, nobody to stifle the sound of their childish laughter, and gradually she relaxed and let herself enjoy the day.

'Mummy, can we have a Christmas tree?' Edward asked as they trudged back for lunch.

More money—not only for the tree, but also for decorations. And she couldn't let herself touch Laura's money except for a house. 'I don't know if we should,' she said, blaming it on the unknown Jake and burying her guilt because she was sick of telling her children that they couldn't have things when it was all because their unprincipled and disinterested father refused to pay up. 'It's not our house, and you know how they drop needles. He might mind.'

'He won't mind! Of course he won't! *Everyone* has a Christmas tree!' Kitty explained patiently to her obviously dense mother.

'But we haven't got the decorations, and anyway, I don't know where we could get one this late,' she said, wondering if she'd get away with it and hating the fact that she had to disappoint them yet again.

They walked on in silence for a moment, then Edward stopped. 'We could make one!' he said, his eyes lighting up at the challenge and finding a solution, as he always did. 'And we could put fir cones on it! There were lots in the wood—and there were some branches there that looked like Christmas tree branches, a bit. Can we get them after lunch and tie them together and pretend they're a tree, and then we can put fir cones on it, and berries—I saw some berries, and I'm sure he won't mind if we only pick a few—'

'Well, he might—'

'No, he won't! Mummy, he's lent us his *house*!' Kitty said earnestly and, not for the first time, Millie felt a stab of unease.

But the children were right, everybody had a tree, and what harm could a few cut branches and some fir cones do? And maybe even the odd sprig of berries…

'All right,' she agreed, 'just a little tree.' So after lunch they trooped back, leaving the exhausted little Rufus snoozing by the fire, and Amelia and Edward loaded themselves up with branches and they set off, Kitty dragging Thomas in the stroller backwards all the way from the woods to the house.

'There!' Edward said in satisfaction, dropping his pile of branches by the back door. 'Now we can make our tree!'

The only thing that kept him going on that hellish journey was the thought of home.

The blissful comfort of his favourite old leather sofa, a bottle of fifteen-year-old single malt and—equally importantly—the painkillers in his flight bag.

Getting upstairs to bed would be beyond him at this point. His knee was killing him—not like last time, when he'd done the ligaments in his other leg, but badly enough to mean that staying would have been pointless, even if he hadn't broken his wrist. And now all he could think about was lying down, and the sooner the better. He'd been stupid to travel so soon; his body was black and blue from end to end, but somehow, with Christmas what felt like seconds away and everyone down in the village getting so damned excited about it, leaving had become imperative now that he could no longer ski to outrun his demons.

Not that he ever really managed to outrun them, although he always gave it a damn good try, but this time he'd come too close to losing everything, and deep down he'd realised that maybe it was time to stop running, time to go home and just get on with life—and at least here he could find plenty to occupy himself.

He heard the car tyres crunch on gravel and cracked open his eyes. Home. Thank God for that. Lights blazed in the dusk, triggered by the taxi pulling up at the door, and handing over what was probably an excessive amount of money, he got out of the car with a grunt of pain and walked slowly to the door.

And stopped.

There was a car on the drive, not one he recognised, and there were lights on inside.

One in the attic, and one on the landing.

'Where d'you want these, guv?' the taxi driver asked, and he glanced down at the cases.

'Just in here would be good,' he said, opening the door and sniffing. Woodsmoke. And there was light coming from the breakfast room, and the sound of—laughter? A child's laughter?

Pain squeezed his chest. Dear God, no. Not today, of all days, when he just needed to crawl into a corner and forget—

'There you go then, guv. Have a good Christmas.'

'And you,' he said, closing the door quietly behind the man and staring numbly towards the breakfast room. What the hell was going on? It must be Kate—no one else had a key, and the place was like Fort Knox. She must have dropped in with Megan and a friend to check on the house—but it didn't sound as if they were checking anything. It sounded as if they were having fun.

Oh, Lord, please, not today…

He limped over to the door and pushed it gently open, and then stood transfixed.

Chaos. Complete, utter chaos.

Two children were sitting on the floor by the fire in a welter of greenery, carefully tying berries to some rather battered branches that looked as if they had come off the conifer hedge at the back of the country club, but it was the woman standing on the table who held his attention.

Tall, slender, with rather wild fair hair escaping from a ponytail and jeans that had definitely seen better days, she was reaching up and twisting another of the branches into the heavy iron hoop over the refectory table, festooning the light fitting with a makeshift attempt at a Christmas decoration which did nothing to improve it.

He'd never seen her before. He would have recognised her, he was sure, if he had. So who the hell—?

His mouth tightened, but then she bent over, giving him an unrestricted view of her neat, shapely bottom as the old jeans pulled across it, and he felt a sudden, unwelcome and utterly unexpected tug of need.

'It's such a shame Jake isn't going to be here, because we're making it so pretty,' the little girl was saying.

'Why *does* he go away?' the boy asked.

'I don't know,' the woman replied, her voice soft and melodious. 'I can't imagine.'

'Didn't Kate say?'

Kate. Of course, she'd be at the bottom of this, he thought, and he could have wrung her neck for her abysmal timing.

Well, if he had two good hands…which at the moment, of course, he didn't.

'He goes skiing.'

'I hate skiing,' the boy said. 'That woman in the kindergarten was horrible. She smelt funny. Here, I've finished this one.'

And he scrambled to his feet and turned round, then caught sight of Jake and froze.

'Well, come on then, give it to me,' the woman said, waving her hand behind her to try and locate it.

'Um…Mum…'

'Darling, give me the branch, I can't stand here for ever—'

She turned towards her son, followed the direction of his gaze and her eyes flew wide. 'Oh—!'

'Mummy, do I need more berries or is that enough?' the little girl asked, but Jake hardly heard her because the woman's eyes were locked on his and the shock and desperation in them blinded his senses to anything else.

'Kitty, hush, darling,' she said softly and, dropping down, she slid off the edge of the table and came towards him with a haphazard attempt at a smile. 'Um…I imagine you're Jake Forrester?' she asked, her voice a little uneven, and he hardened himself against her undoubted appeal and the desperate eyes.

'Well, there you have the advantage over me,' he murmured drily, 'because I have no idea who you are, or why I should come home and find you smothering my house in bits of dead vegetation in my absence—'

Her eyes fluttered briefly closed and colour flooded her cheeks. 'I can explain—'

'Don't bother. I'm not interested. Just get all that—*tat* out of here, clear the place up and then leave.'

He turned on his heel—not a good idea, with his knee screaming in protest, but the pain just fuelled the fire of his anger and he stalked into the study, picked up the phone and rang Kate.

'Millie?'

'So that's her name.'

'*Jake*?' Kate shrieked, and he could hear her collecting herself at the other end of the line. 'What are you doing home?'

'There was an avalanche. I got in the way. And I seem to have guests. Would you care to elaborate?'

'Oh, Jake, I'm so sorry, I can explain—'

'Excellent. Feel free. You've got ten seconds, so make it good.' He settled back in the chair with a wince, listening as Kate sucked in her breath and gave her pitch her best shot.

'She's a friend. Her ex has gone to Thailand, he won't pay the maintenance and she lost her job so she lost her house and her sister kicked her out yesterday.'

'Tough. She's packing now, so I suggest you find some other sucker to put her and her kids up so I can lie and be sore in peace. And don't imagine for a moment that you've heard the end of this.'

He stabbed the off button and threw the phone down on his desk, then glanced up to see the woman—Millie, apparently—transfixed in the doorway, her face still flaming.

'Please don't take it out on Kate. She was only trying to help us.'

He stifled a contemptuous snort and met her eyes challengingly, too sore in every way to moderate his sarcasm. 'You're not doing so well, are you? You don't seem to be able to keep anything. Your husband, your job, your house—even your sister doesn't want you. I wonder why? I wonder what it is about you that makes everyone want to get rid of you?'

She stepped back as if she'd been struck, the colour

draining from her face, and he felt a twinge of guilt but suppressed it ruthlessly.

'We'll be out of here in half an hour. I just need to pack our things. What do you want me to do with the sheets?'

Sheets? He was throwing her out and she was worrying about the *sheets*?

'Just leave them. I wouldn't want to hold you up.'

She straightened her spine and took another step back, and he could see her legs shaking. 'Right. Um…fine.'

And she spun round and walked briskly away in the direction of the breakfast room, leaving him to his guilt. He sighed and sagged back against the chair, a wave of pain swamping him for a moment. When he opened his eyes, the boy was there.

'I'm really sorry,' he said, his little chin up, just like his mother's, his eyes huge in a thin, pale face. 'Please don't be angry with Mummy. She was just trying to make a nice Christmas for us. She thought we were going to stay with Auntie Laura, but Uncle Andy didn't want us there because he said the baby kept him awake—'

There was a baby, too? Dear God, it went from bad to worse, but that wasn't the end of it.

'—and the dog smells and he got on the sofa, and that made him really mad. I heard them fighting. And then Mummy said we were going to see Kate, and she said we ought to come here because you were a nice man and you wouldn't mind and what harm could we do because the house was hundreds of years old and had survived and anyway you liked children or you wouldn't have done the playroom in the attic.'

He finally ran out of breath and Jake stared at him.

Kate thought he was that nice? Kate was dreaming.

But the boy's wounded eyes called to something deep inside him, and Jake couldn't ignore it. Couldn't kick them all out into the cold just before Christmas. Even he wasn't that much of a bastard.

But it wasn't just old Ebenezer Scrooge who had ghosts, and the last thing he needed was a houseful of children over Christmas, Jake thought with a touch of panic. And a baby, of all things, and—a dog?

Not much of a dog. It hadn't barked, and there was no sign of it, so it was obviously a very odd breed of dog. Or old and deaf?

No. Not old and deaf, and not much of a dog at all, he realised, his eyes flicking to the dimly lit hallway behind the boy and focusing on a small red and white bundle of fluff with an anxiously wriggling tail and big soulful eyes that were watching him hopefully.

A little spaniel, like the one his grandmother had had. He'd always liked it—and he wasn't going to be suckered because of the damn dog!

But the boy was still there, one sock-clad foot on top of the other, squirming slightly but holding his ground, and if his ribs hadn't hurt so much he would have screamed with frustration.

'What's your name?'

'Edward. Edward Jones.'

Nice, honest name. Like the child, he thought inconsequentially. Oh, damn. He gave an inward sigh as he felt his defences crumble. After all, it was hardly the boy's fault that he couldn't cope with the memories… 'Where's your mother, Edward?'

'Um…packing. I'm supposed to be clearing up the branches, but I can't reach the ones in the light so I've got to wait for her to come down.'

'Could you go and get her for me, and then look after the others while we have a chat?'

He nodded, but stood there another moment, chewing his lip.

Jake sighed softly. 'What is it?'

'You won't be mean to her, will you? She was only trying to look after us, and she feels so guilty because Dad won't give us any money so we can't have anything nice ever, but it's really not her fault—'

'Just get her, Edward,' he said gently. 'I won't be mean to her.'

'Promise?'

Oh, what was he doing? He needed to get rid of them before he lost his mind! 'I promise.'

The boy vanished, but the dog stayed there, whining softly and wagging his tail, and Jake held out his hand and called the dog over. He came, a little warily, and sat down just a few feet away, tail waving but not yet really ready to trust.

Very wise, Jake thought. He really, really wasn't in a very nice mood, but it was hardly the dog's fault. And he'd promised the boy he wouldn't be mean to his mother.

Well, any more mean than he already had been. He pressed his lips together and sighed. He was going to have to apologise to her, he realised—to the woman who'd moved into his house without a by-your-leave and completely trashed his plans for crawling back into his cave to lick his wounds.

Oh, damn.

'Mummy, he wants to talk to you.'

Millie lifted her head from the bag she was stuffing clothes into and stared at her son. 'I think he's said everything he has to say,' she said crisply. 'Have you finished clearing up downstairs?'

'I couldn't reach the light, but I've put everything else outside and picked up all the bits off the floor. Well, most of them. Mummy, he really does want to talk to you. He asked me to tell you and to look after the others while you have a chat.'

Well, that sounded like a quote, she thought, and her heart sank. It was bad enough enduring the humiliation of one verbal battering. The last thing she needed was to go back down there now he'd drawn breath and had time to think about it and give him the opportunity to have a more concerted attack.

'Please, Mummy. He asked—and he promised he wouldn't be mean to you.'

Her eyes widened, then she shut them fast and counted to ten. What on *earth* had Edward been saying to him? She got to her feet and held out her arms to him, and he ran into them and hugged her hard.

'It'll be all right, Mummy,' he said into her side. 'It will.'

If only she could be so sure.

She let him go and made her way downstairs, down the beautiful old oak staircase she'd fallen so in love with, along the hall on the inches-thick carpet, and tapped on the open study door, her heart pounding out a tattoo against her ribs.

He was sitting with his back to her, and at her knock he swivelled the chair round and met her eyes. He'd taken off the coat that had been slung round his shoulders, and she could see now that he was wearing a cast on his left wrist. And, with the light now shining on his face, she could see the livid bruise on his left cheekbone, and the purple stain around his eye.

His hair was dark, soft and glossy, cut short round the sides but flopping forwards over his eyes. It looked rumpled, as if he'd run his fingers through it over and over again, and his jaw was deeply shadowed. He looks awful, she thought, and she wondered briefly what he'd done.

Not that it mattered. It was enough to have brought him home, and that was the only thing that affected her. His injuries were none of her business.

'You wanted to see me,' she said, and waited for the stinging insults to start again.

'I owe you an apology,' he said gruffly, and she felt her jaw drop and yanked it up again. 'I was unforgivably rude to you, and I had no justification for it.'

'I disagree. I'm in your house without your permission,' she said, fairness overcoming her shock. 'I would have been just as rude, I'm sure.'

'I doubt it, somehow. The manners you've drilled into your son would blow that theory out of the water. He's a credit to you.'

She swallowed hard and nodded. 'Thank you. He's a great kid, and he's been through a lot.'

'I'm sure. However, it's not him I want to talk to you about, it's you. You have nowhere to go, is this right?'

Her chin went up. 'We'll find somewhere,' she lied, her pride rescuing her in the nick of time, and she thought she saw a smile flicker on that strong, sculpted mouth before he firmed it.

'Do you or do you not have anywhere else suitable to go with your children for Christmas?' he asked, a thread of steel underlying the softness of his voice, and she swallowed again and shook her head.

'No,' she admitted. 'But that's not your problem.'

He inclined his head, accepting that, but went on, 'Nevertheless, I do have a problem, and one you might be able to fix. As you can see, I've been stupid enough to get mixed up with an avalanche, and I've broken my wrist. Now, I can't cook at the best of times, and I'm not getting my housekeeper back from her well-earned holiday to wait on me, but you, on the other hand, are here, have nowhere else to go and might therefore be interested in a proposition.'

For the first time, she felt a flicker of hope. 'A proposition?' she asked warily, not quite sure she liked the sound of that but prepared to listen because her options were somewhat limited. He nodded.

'I have no intention of paying you—under the circumstances, I don't think that's unreasonable, considering you moved into my house without my knowledge or consent and made yourselves at home, but I am prepared to let you stay until such time as you find somewhere to go after the New Year, in exchange for certain duties. Can you cook?'

She felt the weight of fear lift from her shoulders, and

nodded. 'Yes, I can cook,' she assured him, hoping she could still remember how. It was a while since she'd had anything lavish on her table, but cooking had once been her love and her forte.

'Good. You can cook for me, and keep the housework under control, and help me do anything I can't manage—can you drive?'

She nodded again. 'Yes—but it will have to be my car, unless you've got a big one. I can't go anywhere without the children, so if it's some sexy little sports car it will have to be my hatchback.'

'I've got an Audi A6 estate. It's automatic. Is that a problem?'

'No problem,' she said confidently. 'David had one.' On a finance agreement that, like everything else, had gone belly-up in the last few years. 'Anything else? Any rules?'

'Yes. The children can use the playroom upstairs on the landing, and you can keep the attic bedrooms—I assume you're in the three with the patchwork quilts?'

She felt her jaw sag. 'How did you guess?'

His mouth twisted into a wry smile. 'Let's just say I'm usually a good judge of character, and you're pretty easy to read,' he told her drily. 'So—you can have the top floor, and when you're cooking the children can be down here in the breakfast room with you.'

'Um…there's the dog,' she said, a little unnecessarily as Rufus was now sitting on her foot, and to her surprise Jake's mouth softened into a genuine smile.

'Yes,' he said quietly. 'The dog. My grandmother had one like him. What's his name?'

'Rufus,' she said, and the little dog's tail wagged hope-fully. 'Please don't say he has to be outside in a kennel or anything awful, because he's old and not very well and it's so cold at the moment and he's no trouble—'

'Millie—what does that stand for, by the way?'

'Amelia.'

He studied her for a second, then nodded. 'Amelia,' he said, his voice turning it into something that sounded almost like a caress. 'Of course the dog doesn't have to be outside—not if he's housetrained.'

'Oh, he is. Well, mostly. Sometimes he has the odd accident, but that's only if he's ill.'

'Fine. Just don't let him on the beds. Right, I'm done. If you could find me a glass, the malt whisky and my flight bag, I'd be very grateful. And then I'm going to lie down on my sofa and go to sleep.'

And, getting to his feet with a grunt of pain, he limped slowly towards her.

'You really did mess yourself up, didn't you?' she said softly, and he paused just a foot away from her and stared down into her eyes for the longest moment.

'Yes, Amelia. I really did—and I could do with those painkillers, so if you wouldn't mind—?'

'Right away,' she said, trying to remember how to breathe. Slipping past him into the kitchen, she found a glass, filled it with water, put the kettle on, made a sandwich with the last of the cheese and two precious slices of bread, smeared some chutney she found in the fridge onto the cheese and took it through to him.

'I thought you might be hungry,' she said, 'and there's

nothing much else in the house at the moment, but you shouldn't take painkillers on an empty stomach.'

He sighed and looked up at her from the sofa where he was lying stretched out full length and looking not the slightest bit vulnerable despite the cast, the bruises and the swelling under his eye. 'Is that right?' he said drily. 'Where's the malt whisky?'

'You shouldn't have alcohol—'

'—with painkillers,' he finished for her, and gave a frustrated growl that probably should have frightened her but just gave her the urge to smile. 'Well, give me the damned painkillers, then. They're in my flight bag, in the outside pocket. I'll take them with the water.'

She rummaged, found them and handed them to him. 'When did you take the last lot? It says no more than six in twenty-four hours—'

'Did I ask you for your medical advice?' he snarled, taking the strip of tablets from her and popping two out awkwardly with his good hand.

Definitely not vulnerable. Just crabby as hell. She stood her ground. 'I just don't want your family suing me for killing you with an overdose,' she said, and his mouth tightened.

'No danger of that,' he said flatly. 'I don't have a family. Now, go away and leave me alone. I haven't got the energy to argue with a mouthy, opinionated woman and I can't stand being fussed over. And find me the whisky!'

'I've put the kettle on to make you tea or coffee—'

'Well, don't bother. I've had enough caffeine in the last twenty-four hours to last me a lifetime. I just want the malt—'

'Eat the sandwich and I'll think about it,' she said, and then went out and closed the door, quickly, before he changed his mind and threw them all out anyway...

CHAPTER THREE

EDWARD was waiting for her.

He was sitting on the top step, and his eyes were full of trepidation. 'Well?'

'We're staying,' she said with a smile, still not really believing it but so out of options that she had to *make* it work. 'But he'd like us to spend the time up here unless we're down in the breakfast room or kitchen cooking for him, so we don't disturb him, because he had an accident skiing and he's a bit sore. He needs to sleep.'

'So can I unpack my things again?' Kitty asked, appearing on the landing, her little face puzzled and a bulging carrier bag dangling from her fingers.

'Yes, darling. We can all unpack, and then we need to go downstairs very quietly and tidy up the kitchen and see what I can find to cook us for supper.'

Not that there was much, but she'd have to make something proper for Jake, and she had no idea how she'd achieve that with no ingredients and no money to buy any. Maybe there was something in his freezer?

'I'll be very, very quiet,' Kitty whispered, her grey eyes

serious, and tiptoed off to her room with bag in hand and her finger pressed over her lips.

It worked until she bumped into the door frame and the bag fell out of her hand and landed on the floor, the book in the top falling out with a little thud. Her eyes widened like saucers, and for one awful minute Millie thought she was going to cry.

'It's all right, darling, you don't have to be that quiet,' she said with an encouraging smile, and Edward, ever his little sister's protector, picked up his own bag and went back into the bedroom and hugged her, then helped her put her things away while Millie unpacked all the baby's things again.

He was still sleeping. Innocence was such a precious gift, she thought, her eyes filling, and blinking hard, she turned away and went to the window, drawn by the sound of a car. Looking down on the drive as the floodlights came on, she realised it was Kate.

Of course. Dear Kate, rushing to her rescue, coming to smooth things over with Jake.

Who was sleeping.

'Keep an eye on Thomas, I'm going to let Kate in,' she said to Edward and ran lightly down the stairs, arriving in the hall just as Kate turned the heavy handle and opened the door.

'Oh, Millie, I'm so sorry I've been so long, but Megan was in the bath and I had to dry her hair before I brought her out in the cold,' she said in a rush. 'Where are the children?'

'Upstairs. It's all right, we're staying. Megan, do you

want to go up and see them while I make Mummy a coffee?'

'I don't have time for a coffee, I need to see Jake. I've got to try and reason with him—what do you mean, you're staying?' she added, her eyes widening.

'Shh. He's asleep. Go on, Megan, it's all right, but please be quiet because Jake's not well.'

Megan nodded seriously. 'I'll be very quiet,' she whispered and ran upstairs, her little feet soundless on the thick carpet. Kate took Millie by the arm and towed her into the breakfast room and closed the door.

'So what's going on?' she asked in a desperate undertone. 'I thought you'd be packed and leaving?'

Amelia shook her head. 'No. He's broken his wrist and he's battered from end to end, and I think he's probably messed his knee up, too, so he needs someone to cook for him and run round after him.'

Kate's jaw dropped. 'So he's *employing* you?'

Millie felt her mouth twist into a wry smile. 'Not exactly employing,' she admitted, remembering his blunt words with an inward wince. 'But we can stay in exchange for helping him, so long as I keep the children out of his way.'

'And the dog? Does he even *know* about the dog?'

She smiled. 'Ah, well, now. Apparently he likes the dog, doesn't he, Rufus?' she murmured, looking down at him. He was stuck on her leg, sensing the need to behave, his eyes anxious, and she felt him quiver.

When she glanced back up, Kate was staring at her openmouthed. 'He likes the dog?' she hissed.

'His grandmother had one. He doesn't go a bundle on the Christmas decorations, though,' she added ruefully with a pointed glance at the light fitting. 'Come on, let's make a drink and take it upstairs to the kids.'

'He was going to put a kitchen up there,' Kate told her as she boiled the kettle. 'Just a little one, enough to make drinks and snacks, but he hasn't got round to it yet. Pity. It would have been handy for you.'

'It would. Still, I only need to bring the children down if I'm actually cooking. We're quite all right up in the playroom, and at least it'll give us a little breathing space before we have to find somewhere to go.'

'And, actually, it's a huge relief,' Kate said, sagging back against the worktop and folding her arms. 'I was wondering what to do about Jake—I mean, I couldn't leave him here on his own over Christmas when he's injured, but my house is going to be heaving and noisy and chaotic, and I would have had to run backwards and forwards—so you've done me a massive favour. And, you never know, maybe you'll all have a good time together! In fact—'

Amelia cut her off with a laugh and a raised hand. 'I don't think so,' she said firmly, remembering his bitterly sarcastic opening remarks. 'But if we can just keep out of his way, maybe we'll all survive.'

She handed Kate her drink, picked up her own mug and then hesitated. No matter how rude and sarcastic he'd been, he was still a human being and for that alone he deserved her consideration, and he was injured and exhausted and probably not thinking straight. 'I ought to check on him,' she said, putting her mug back down. 'He was talking about malt whisky.'

'So? Don't worry, he's not a drinker. He won't have had much.'

'On top of painkillers?'

'Ah. What were they?'

'Goodness knows—something pretty heavy-duty. Nothing I recognised. Not paracetamol, that's for sure!'

'Oh, hell. Where is he?'

'Just next door in the little sitting room.'

'I'll go—'

'No. Let me. He was pretty cross.'

Kate laughed softly. 'You think I've never seen him cross?'

So they went together, opening the door silently and pushing it in until they could see him sprawled full length on the sofa, one leg dangling off the edge, his cast resting across his chest, his head lolling against the arm.

Kate frowned. 'He doesn't look very comfortable.'

He didn't, but at least there was no sign of the whisky. Amelia went into the room and picked up a soft velvety cushion and tucked it under his bruised cheek to support his head better. He grunted and shifted slightly and she froze, waiting for those piercing slate grey eyes to open and stab her with a hard, angry glare, but then he relaxed, settling his face down against the pillow with a little sigh, and she let herself breathe again.

It was chilly in there, though, and she had refused to let Kate turn the heating up. She could do it now but, in the meantime, he ought to have something over him. She spotted a throw over the back of the other sofa and lowered it carefully over him, tucking it in to keep the draughts off until the heat kicked in.

Then she tiptoed out, glancing back over her shoulder as she reached the door.

Did she imagine it or had his eyelids fluttered? She wasn't sure, but she didn't want to hang around and provoke him if she'd disturbed him, so she pushed Kate out and closed the door softly behind them.

'Can you turn the heating up?' she murmured to Kate, and she nodded and went into his study and fiddled with a keypad on the wall.

'He looks awful,' Kate said, sparing the door of the room another glance as she tapped keys and reprogrammed the heating. 'He's got bruises all over his face and neck. It must have been a hell of an avalanche.'

'He didn't say, but he's very sore and stiff. I expect he's got bruises all over his body,' Millie said, trying not to think about his body in too much detail but failing dismally. She stifled the little whimper that rose in her throat.

Why?

Why, of all the men to bring her body out of the freezer, did it have to be Jake? There was no way he'd be interested in her—even if she hadn't upset and alienated him by taking such a massive liberty with his house, to all intents and purposes moving into his house as a squatter, she'd then compounded her sins by telling him what to do!

And he most particularly wouldn't be interested in her children. In fact it was probably the dog who was responsible for his change of heart.

Oh, well, it was just as well he wouldn't be interested in her, because there was no way her life was even remotely stable or coherent enough at the moment for her to contemplate a relationship. Frankly, she wasn't sure it ever would be again and, if it was, it *certainly* wouldn't be with another empire builder. She'd had it with the entrepreneurial type, big time.

But there was just something about Jake Forrester that called to something deep inside her, something that had lain undisturbed for years, and she was going to have to ignore it and get through these next few days and weeks until they could find somewhere else. And maybe then she'd get her sanity back.

'Come on, let's go back up and leave him to sleep,' she said, crossing her fingers and hoping that he slept for a good long while and woke in a rather better mood…

He was hot.

He'd been cold, but he'd been too tired and sore to bother to get the throw, but someone must have been in and covered him, because it was snuggled round him, and there was a pillow under his face and the lingering scent of a familiar fragrance.

Kate. She must have come over and covered him up. Hell. He hadn't meant her to turn out on such a freezing night with little Megan. He should have rung her back, he realised, after he'd spoken to Amelia, but he'd been high as a kite on the rather nice drugs the French doctor had given him and he hadn't even thought about it.

Damn.

He rolled onto his back and his breath caught. Ouch. That was quite a bruise on his left hip. And his knee desperately needed some ice, and his arm hurt. Even through the painkillers.

He struggled off the sofa, eventually escaping from the confines of the throw with an impatient tug and straightening up with a wince. The gel pack was in the freezer in the kitchen. It wasn't far.

Further than he thought, he realised, swaying slightly and pausing while the world steadied. He took a step, then another, and blinked hard to clear his head.

Amelia was right, he shouldn't have too many of those damn painkillers. They were turning his brain to mush. And it was probably just as well he hadn't taken them with whisky either, he thought with regret. Not that she'd been about to give him any, the bossy witch.

Amelia. Millie.

No, Amelia. Millie didn't suit her. It was a little girl's name and, whatever else she was, she was all woman. And damn her for making him notice the fact.

He limped into the breakfast room and saw that Edward had done a pretty good job of removing the branches and berries from the floor in front of the fire. He felt his brow pleat into a frown, and stifled the pang of guilt. It was his house. If he didn't want decorations in it, it was perfectly reasonable to say so.

But had he had to be so harsh?

No, was the simple answer. Especially to the kids. Oh, rats. He made his way carefully through to the kitchen, took the pack out of the freezer and wrapped it in a tea towel, then went back to the breakfast room and sat down in the chair near the fire and propped the ice pack over his knee. Better.

Or it would be, in about a week. It was only a bruise, not a ligament rupture, thankfully. He'd done that before on the other knee, and he didn't need to do it again, but he realised he'd been lucky not to be smashed to bits on the tree or the rock field.

Very lucky.

He eased back in the chair cautiously and thought with longing of the whisky. It was a particularly smooth old single malt, smoky and peaty, with a lovely complex after-taste. Or was that afterburn?

Whatever, it was in the drinks cupboard in the drawing room, and he wasn't convinced he could summon up the energy to walk all the way to the far end of the house and back again, so he closed his eyes and fantasised that he was on Islay, sitting in an old croft house with a peat fire at his feet, a collie instead of a little spaniel leaning on his leg and a glass of liquid gold in his hand.

He could all but taste it. Pity he couldn't. Pity it was only in his imagination, because then he'd be able to put Amelia and her children out of his mind.

Or he would have been able to, if it hadn't been for the baby crying.

'Oh, Thomas, sweetheart, what's the matter, little one?'

She couldn't believe he was doing this. She'd fed him just before Jake had arrived home, but now he was awake and he wouldn't settle again and he was starting to sob into her chest, letting fly with a scream that she was sure would travel all the way down to Jake.

He couldn't be hungry, not really, but he obviously wanted a bottle of milk, and that meant going back down to the kitchen and heating it, taking the screaming baby with her, and by the time she'd done that, he would certainly have disturbed her reluctant host. Unless she left him with Edward?

'Darling, could you please look after him for a moment while I get him his bottle?' she asked, and Edward, being Edward, just nodded and held his arms out, and carried Thomas off towards the bedroom and closed the door.

She ran lightly downstairs to the sound of his escalating wails. As she hurried into the breakfast room, she came face to face with Jake sitting by the fire, an ice pack on his knee and the dog at his side.

She skidded to a halt and his eyes searched her face. 'Is the baby all right?'

She nodded. 'Yes—I'm sorry. I just need to make him a bottle. He'll settle then. I'm really sorry—'

'Why didn't you bring him down?'

'I didn't want to wake you.' She chewed her lip, only too conscious of the fact that he was very much awake. Awake and up and about and looking rumpled and disturbingly attractive, with the dark shadow of stubble on his firm jaw and the subtle drift of a warm, slightly spicy cologne reaching her nostrils.

'I was awake,' he told her, his voice a little gruff. 'I put a gel pack on my knee, and I was about to make some tea. Want to join me?'

'Oh—I can't, I've left the baby with Edward.'

'Bring them all down. Maybe I should meet them—since they're staying in my house.'

Oh, Lord. 'Let me just make the bottle so it can be cooling, and then we'll get a little peace and I can introduce you properly.'

He nodded, his mouth twitching into a slight smile, and she felt relief flood through her at this tiny evidence of his humanity. She went into the kitchen and spooned formula into a bottle, then poured hot water from the kettle on it, shook it and plonked it into a bowl of cold water. Thankfully there had been some water in the kettle so it didn't have to cool from boiling, she thought as she ran back upstairs and collected the children, suddenly ludicrously conscious of how scruffy they looked after foraging in the woods, and how apprehensive.

'Hey, it's all right, he wants to meet you,' she murmured reassuringly to Kitty, who was clinging to her, and then pushed the breakfast room door open and ushered them in.

He was putting wood on the fire, and as he closed the door and straightened up, he caught sight of them and turned. The smile was gone, his face oddly taut, and her own smile faltered for a moment.

'Kids, this is Mr Forrester—'

'Jake,' he said, cutting her off and taking a step forward. His mouth twisted into a smile. 'I've already met Edward. And you must be Kitty. And this, I take it, is Thomas?'

'Yes.'

Thomas, sensing the change of atmosphere, had gone obligingly silent, but after a moment he lost interest in Jake and anything except his stomach and, burrowing into her shoulder, he began to wail again.

'I'm sorry. I—'

'Go on, feed him. I gave the bottle a shake to help cool it.'

'Thanks.' She went into the kitchen, wondering how he knew to do that. Nieces and nephews, probably—although he'd said he didn't have any family. How odd, she thought briefly, but then Thomas tried to lunge out of her arms and she fielded him with the ease of practice and tested the bottle on her wrist.

Cool enough. She shook it again, tested it once more to be on the safe side and offered it to her son.

Silence. Utter, blissful silence, broken only by a strained chuckle.

'Oh, for such simple needs,' he said softly, and she turned and met his eyes. They were darker than before, and his mouth was set in a grim line despite the laugh. But then his expression went carefully blank and he limped across to the kettle. 'So—who has tea, and who wants juice or whatever else?'

'We haven't got any juice. The children will have water.'

'Sounds dull.'

'They're fine with it. It's good for them.'

'I don't doubt it. It's good for me, too, but that doesn't mean I drink it. Except in meetings. I get through gallons of it in meetings. So—is that just me, or are you going to join me?'

'Oh.' Join him? That sounded curiously—intimate. 'Yes, please,' she said, and hoped she didn't sound absurdly breathless. It's a cup of tea, she told herself crossly. Just a cup of tea. Nothing else. She didn't want anything else. Ever.

And if she told herself that enough times, maybe she'd start to believe it.

'Have the children eaten?'

'Thomas has. Edward and Kitty haven't. I was going to wait until you woke up and ask you what you wanted.'

'Anything. I'm not really hungry after that sandwich. What is there?'

'I have no idea. I'll give the children eggs on toast—'

'Again?' Kitty said plaintively. 'We had eggs on toast for supper last night.'

'I'm sure we can find something else,' their host was saying, rummaging in a tall cupboard with pull-out racking that was crammed with tins and jars and packets. 'What did you all have for lunch?'

'Jam sandwiches and an apple.'

He turned and studied Kitty thoughtfully, then his gaze flicked up to Amelia's and speared her. 'Jam sandwiches?' he said softly. 'Eggs on toast?'

She felt her chin lift, but he just frowned and turned back to the cupboard, staring into its depths blankly for a moment before shutting it and opening the big door beside it and going systematically through the drawers of the freezer.

'How about fish?'

'What sort? They don't eat smoked fish or fish fingers.'

'Salmon—and mixed shellfish. A lobster,' he added, rummaging. 'Raw king prawns—there's some Thai curry paste somewhere I just saw. Or there's probably a casserole if you don't fancy fish.'

'Whatever. Choose what you want. We'll have eggs.'

He frowned again, shut the freezer and studied her searchingly.

She wished he wouldn't do that. Her arm was aching, Thomas was starting to loll against her shoulder and if she was sitting down, she could probably settle him and get him off to sleep so she could concentrate on feeding the others—most particularly their reluctant host.

After all, she'd told him she could cook—

'Go and sit down. I'll order a takeaway,' he said softly, and she looked back up into his eyes and surprised a gentle, almost puzzled expression in them for a fleeting moment before he turned away and limped out. 'What do they like?' he asked over his shoulder, then turned to the children. 'What's it to be, kids? Pizza? Chinese? Curry? Kebabs? Burgers?'

'What's a kebab?'

'Disgusting. Anyway, you're having eggs, Kitty, we've already decided that.'

Over their heads she met his eyes defiantly, and saw a reluctant grin blossom on his firm, sculpted lips. 'OK, we'll have eggs. Do we have enough?'

We? Her eyes widened. 'For all of us?'

'Am I excluded?'

She ran a mental eye over the meagre contents of the fridge and relaxed. 'Of course not.'

'Good. Then we'll have omelettes and oven-baked potato wedges and peas, if that's OK? Now, for heaven's sake sit down, woman, before you drop the baby, and I'll make you a cup of tea.'

'I thought I was supposed to be looking after you?' she said, but one glare from those rather gorgeous slate grey eyes and she retreated to the comfort of the fireside, settling down in the chair he'd been using with a sigh of relief. She'd have her tea, settle Thomas in his cot and make supper.

For all of them, apparently. So—was he going to sit and eat with them? He'd been so anti his little army of squatters, so what had brought about this sudden change?

* * *

Jake pulled the mugs out of the cupboard and then contemplated the lid of the tea caddy. Tea bags, he decided, with only one useful hand, not leaves and the pot, and putting the caddy back, he dropped tea bags into the mugs and poured water on them. Thank God it was his left arm he'd broken, not his right. At least he could manage most things like this.

The stud on his jeans was a bit of a challenge, he'd discovered, but he'd managed to get them on this morning. Shoelaces were another issue, but he'd kicked his shoes off when he'd got in and he'd been padding around in his socks, and he had shoes without laces he could wear until the blasted cast came off.

But cooking—well, cooking would be a step too far, he thought, but by some minor intervention of fate he seemed to have acquired an answer to that one. A feisty, slightly offbeat and rather delightful answer. Easy on the eye. And with a voice that seemed to dig right down inside him and tug at something long forgotten.

It was the kids he found hardest, of course, but it was the kids he was most concerned about, because their mother was obviously struggling to hold things together. And she wasn't coping very well with it—or maybe, he thought, reconsidering as he poked the tea bags with the spoon, she was coping very well, against atrocious odds. Whatever, a staple diet of bread and eggs wasn't good for anyone and, as he knew from his experience with the cheese sandwich, it wasn't even decent bread. Perfectly nutritious, no doubt, but closely related to cotton wool.

He put the milk down and poured two glasses of filtered water for Edward and Kitty. 'Hey, you guys, come and get your drinks,' he said, and they ran over, Edward more slowly, Kitty skipping, head on one side in a gesture so like her mother's he nearly laughed.

'So—what *are* kebabs, really?' she asked, twizzling a lock of hair with one forefinger, and he did laugh then, the sound dragged out of him almost reluctantly.

'Well—there are different kinds. There's shish kebab, which is pieces of meat on skewers, a bit like you'd put on a barbecue, or there's doner kebab, which is like a great big sausage on a stick, and they turn it in front of a fire to cook it and slice bits off. You have both in a kind of bread pocket, with salad, and your mother's right, the doner kebabs certainly aren't very healthy—well, not the ones in this country. In Turkey they're fantastic.'

'They don't *sound* disgusting,' Kitty said wistfully. 'I like sausages on sticks.'

'Maybe we can get some sausages and put sticks in them,' Edward said, and Jake realised he was the peacemaker in the family, trying to hold it all together, humouring Kitty and helping with Thomas and supporting his mother—and the thought that he should have to do all that left a great hollow in the pit of Jake's stomach.

No child should have to do that. He'd spent years doing that, fighting helplessly against the odds to keep it all together, and for what?

'Good idea,' he said softly. 'We'll get some sausages tomorrow.' He gathered up the mugs in his right hand and limped through to the breakfast room and put them down on the table near Amelia. She looked up with a smile.

'Thanks,' she murmured, and he found his eyes drawn down to the baby, sleeping now, his chubby little face turned against her chest, arm outflung, dead to the world. A great lump in his throat threatened to choke him, and he nodded curtly, took his mug and went back to the other room, shutting the door firmly so he couldn't hear the children's voices.

He couldn't do this. It was killing him, and he couldn't do it.

He'd meant to sit with her, talk to her, but the children had unravelled him and he couldn't sit there and look at them, he discovered. Not today. Not the day before Christmas Eve.

The day his wife and son had died.

CHAPTER FOUR

WELL, what was that about?

He'd come in, taken one look at her and gone.

Because she'd sat in his chair?

No—and he'd been looking at Thomas, not her. And had she dreamed it, or had there been a slight sheen in his eyes?

The glitter of tears?

No. She was being ridiculous. He just wanted to be alone. He always wanted to be alone, according to Kate, and they'd scuppered that for him, so he was making the best of a bad job and keeping out of the way.

So why did he want to eat with them? Or was he simply having the same food?

She had no idea, and no way of working it out, and knowing so little about him, her guesswork was just a total stab in the dark. But there had been *something* in his eyes...

'I'm just going to put Thomas to bed, then I'll cook you supper,' she told the children quietly and, getting up without disturbing the baby, she took him up to the attic and slipped him into his cot. She'd change his nappy later.

She didn't want to risk waking him now—not when he'd finally settled.

And not when Jake had that odd look about him that was flagging up all kinds of warning signals. She was sure he was hurting, but she had no idea why—and it was frankly none of her business. She just needed to feed the children, get them out of the way and then deal with him later.

'Right, kids, let's make supper,' she said, going back in and smiling at them brightly. 'Who wants to break the eggs into the cup?'

Not the bowl, because that was just asking for trouble, and she sensed that crunchy omelettes wouldn't win her any Brownie points with Jake, but one at a time was all right. She could fish for shell in one egg.

She looked out of the window at the herb garden and wondered what was out there. Sage? Rosemary? Thyme? It was a shame she didn't have any cheese, but she could put fresh herbs in his, and she remembered seeing a packet of pancetta in the fridge.

She cooked for herself and the children first, then while she was eating she cooked his spicy potato wedges in a second batch, then sent the children up to wash and change ready for bed.

'I'll come up and read to you when I've given Jake his supper,' she promised, kissing them both, and they went, still looking a little uncertain, and she felt another wave of anger at David for putting them in this position.

And at herself, for allowing him to make them so vulnerable, for relying on him even after he'd proved over and over again that he was unreliable, for giving him the power to do this to them. He'd walked out on them four years ago, and letting him back again two years later had been stupid in the extreme. It hadn't taken her long to realise it, and she'd finally taken the last step and divorced him, but their failed reconciliation had resulted in Thomas. And, though she loved Thomas to bits, having him didn't make life easier and had forced her to rely on David again. Well, no more. Not him, not any man.

Never again, she thought, vigorously beating the last two eggs for Jake's omelette while the little cubes of pancetta crisped in the pan. No way was she putting herself and her family at risk again. Even if Jake was remotely interested in her, which he simply wasn't. He couldn't even bear to be in the same room as her—and she had to stop thinking about him!

She went out and picked the herbs by the light from the kitchen window, letting Rufus out into the garden for a moment while she breathed deeply and felt the cold, clean air fill her lungs and calm her.

They'd survive, she told herself. They'd get through this hitch, and she'd get another job somehow, and they'd be all right.

They had to be.

She went back in with Rufus and the herbs, made Jake's omelette and left it to set on the side of the Aga while she called him to the table.

She tapped on the door of what she was beginning to think of as his cave, and he opened it almost instantly. She stepped back hastily and smiled. 'Hi. I was just coming to call you for supper.'

He smiled back. 'The smell was reeling me in—I was just on my way. Apparently I'm hungrier than I thought.'

Oh, damn. Had she made enough for him?

He followed her through to the breakfast room and stopped. 'Where are the other place settings?'

'Oh—the children were starving, so I ate with them. Anyway, I wasn't sure—'

She broke off, biting her lip, and he sighed softly.

'I'm sorry. I was rude. I just walked out.'

'No—no, why should you want to sit with us? It's your house, we're in your way. I feel so guilty—'

'Don't. Please, don't. I don't know the ins and outs of it, and I don't need to, but it's quite obvious that you're doing your best to cope and life's just gone pear-shaped recently. And, whatever the rights and wrongs of your being here, it's nothing to do with the children. They've got every right to feel safe and secure, and wanted, and if I've given you the impression that they're not welcome here, then I apologise. I don't do kids—I have my reasons, which I don't intend to go into, but—your kids have done nothing wrong and—well, tomorrow I'd like to fix it a bit, if you'll let me.'

'Fix it?' she said, standing with the plate in her hand and her eyes searching his. 'How?' How on earth could he fix it? And why didn't he do kids?

'I'd like to give the children Christmas. I'd like to go shopping and buy food. I've already promised them sausages, but I'd like to get the works—a turkey and all the trimmings, satsumas, mince pies, Christmas cake, a Christmas pudding and cream, and something else if they don't like the heavy fruit—perhaps a chocolate log or something? And a tree. They ought to have a tree, with real decorations on it.'

She felt her eyes fill with tears, and swallowed hard.

'You don't have to do that,' she said, trying to firm her voice. 'We don't need all that.'

'I know—but I'd like to. I don't normally do Christmas, but the kids have done nothing to deserve this hideous uncertainty in their lives, and if I can help to make this time a little better for them, then maybe—'

He broke off and turned away, moving slowly to the table, his leg obviously troubling him.

She set the plate down in front of him with trembling hands. 'I don't know what to say.'

'Then just say yes, and let me do it,' he said gruffly, then tilted his head and gave her a wry look. 'I don't suppose I'm allowed a glass of wine?'

'Of course you are.'

'You wouldn't let me have the whisky.'

She gave a little laugh, swallowing down the tears and shaking her head. 'That was because of the painkillers. I thought you should drink water, especially as you'd been flying. But—sure, you can have a glass of wine.'

'Will you join me?'

'I thought you wanted to be alone?' she said softly, and he smiled again, a little crookedly.

'Amelia, just open the wine. There's a gluggable Aussie Shiraz in the wine rack in the side of the island unit, and the glasses are in the cupboard next to the Aga.'

'Corkscrew?'

'It's a screwtop.'

'Right.' She found the wine, found the glasses, poured his and a small one for herself and perched a little warily opposite him. 'How's the omelette?'

'Good. Just right. What herbs did you use? Are they from the garden?'

'Yes. Thyme and sage. And I found some pancetta—I hope it was OK to use it.'

'Of course. It's really tasty. Thanks.'

He turned his attention back to his food, and then pushed his plate away with a sigh when it was scraped clean. 'I don't suppose there's any pud?'

She chuckled. 'A budget yogurt?'

He wrinkled his nose. 'Maybe not. There might be some ice cream in the freezer—top drawer.'

There was. Luxury Belgian chocolate that made her mouth water. 'This one?' she offered, and he nodded.

'Brilliant. Will you join me?'

She gave in to the temptation because her omelette had only been tiny—elastic eggs, to make sure he had enough so she didn't fall at the first hurdle—and she was still hungry. She dished up and took it through, feeling a pang of guilt because she could feed her children for a day on the cost of that ice cream and in the good old days it had been their favourite—

'Stop it. We'll get some for the children tomorrow,' he chided, reading her mind with uncanny accuracy, and she laughed and sat down.

'How did you know?'

His mouth quirked. 'Your face is like an open book—every flicker of guilt registers on it. Stop beating yourself up, Amelia, and tell me about yourself. What do you do for a living?'

She tried to smile, but it felt pretty pathetic, really. 'Nothing at the moment. I was working freelance as a technical translator for a firm that went into liquidation. They owed me for three months' work.'

'Ouch.'

'Indeed. And David had just run off to Thailand with the receivers in hot pursuit after yet another failed business venture—'

'David?'

'My ex-husband. Self-styled entrepreneur and master of delusion, absent father of my children and what Kate describes as a waste of a good skin. He'd already declined to pay the maintenance when I left him for the second time when I was pregnant with Thomas, so I'd already had to find a way to survive for over a year while I waited for the courts to tell him to pay up. And then I lost my job, David wasn't in a position to help by then even if he'd chosen to, and my landlord wanted out of the property business so the moment I couldn't pay my overdue rent on the date he'd set, he asked me to leave. As in, "I want you out by the morning".'

Jake winced. 'So you went to your sister.'

'Yes. We moved in on the tenth of December—and it lasted less than two weeks.' She laughed softly and wrinkled her nose. 'You know what they say about guests being like fish—they go off after three days. So twelve wasn't bad. And the dog does smell.'

'So why don't you bath him?'

'Because they wouldn't let me. Not in their pristine house. I would have had to take him to the groomer, which I couldn't afford, or do it outside under the hose.'

'In December?' he said with a frown.

She smiled wryly, remembering Andy's blank incomprehension. 'Quite. So he still smells, I'm afraid.'

'That's ridiculous. Heavens, he's only tiny. Shove him in the sink and dry him by the fire.'

'Really?' She put down her ice cream spoon and sat back, staring at him in amazement. 'You're telling me I could bath him in your lovely kitchen?'

'Why not? Or you could use the utility room. Wherever. It doesn't matter, does it? He's only a dog. I can think of worse things. You're all right, aren't you, mate?' he said softly, turning his head and looking at the hearth where Rufus was lying as close to the woodburner as the fireguard would let him. He thumped his tail on the floor, his eyes fixed on Jake as if he was afraid that any minute now he'd be told to move.

But apparently not. Jake liked dogs—and thought it was fine to wash him in the kitchen sink. She stood up and took their bowls through to the kitchen, using the excuse to get away because her eyes were filling again and threatening to overflow and embarrass her. She put all the plates into the dishwasher and straightened up and took a nice steadying breath.

Rufus was at her feet, his tail waving, his eyes hopeful.

She had to squash the urge to hug him. 'Do you think I'm going to give you something? You've had supper,' she told him firmly. 'Don't beg.'

His tail drooped and he trotted back to Jake and sat beside him, staring up into his eyes and making him laugh.

'He's not looking convinced.'

'Don't you dare give him anything. He's not allowed to beg, and he's on a special diet.'

'I don't doubt it. I bet he costs more to run than all the rest of you put together.'

She laughed and shook her head. 'You'd better believe it. But he's worth every penny. He's been brilliant.' She bit her lip. 'I don't mean to be rude, but I did promise the children I'd read to them, and I need to change Thomas's nappy and put him into pyjamas.'

He nodded. 'That's fine. Don't worry. I'll see you later. In fact, I might just go to bed.'

'Can I get you anything else?'

He shook his head. 'No. I'm fine, don't worry about me. I'll see you in the morning. If you get a minute before then, you could dream up a shopping list. And thank you for my supper, by the way, it was lovely.'

She felt the cold, dead place around her heart warm a little, and she smiled. 'My pleasure,' she said, and took herself upstairs before she fell any further under his spell, because she'd discovered during the course of a glass of wine and a bowl of ice cream that Jake Forrester, when it suited him, could be very, very charming indeed.

And that scared the living daylights out of her.

His bags were missing.

The cabbie had stacked them by the front door, and they were gone. Kate, he thought. She'd been over while he was sleeping earlier, he knew that, and he realised she must have taken them up to his room. Unless Amelia had done it?

Whatever, he needed to go to bed. Lying on the sofa resting for an hour was all very well, but he needed more than that. And it was already after ten. He'd sat and had another glass of wine in front of the fire in the breakfast room, with Rufus keeping him company and creeping gradually closer until he was lying against his foot, and eventually it dawned on him that he was hanging around in the vain hope that Amelia would come back down and sit with him again.

Ridiculous. And dangerous. They both had far too much baggage, and it would be dicing with disaster, no matter how appealing the physical package. And there was no way he wanted any other kind of relationship. So, although he was loath to disturb the dog, he'd finally eased his toes out from under his side and left the room.

And then had to work out, in his muddled, tired mind, what had happened to his bags.

He detoured into the sitting room and picked up his painkillers, then made his way slowly and carefully up the stairs. He was getting stiffer, he realised. Maybe he needed a bath—a long, hot soak—except that he'd almost inevitably fall asleep in it and wake up cold and wrinkled in the middle of the night. And, anyway, he hated baths.

A shower? No. There was the difficulty of his cast to consider, and sealing it in a bag was beyond him at the moment. He'd really had enough. He'd deal with it tomorrow.

Reluctantly abandoning the tempting thought of hot water sluicing over his body, he eased off his clothes, found his wash things in the bag that had indeed arrived in his room, cleaned his teeth and then crawled into bed.

Bliss.

There was nothing like your own bed, he thought, closing his eyes with a long, unravelling sigh. And then he remembered he hadn't taken the painkillers, and he needed to before he went to sleep or his arm would wake him in the night.

He put the light back on and got out of bed again, filled a glass with water and came back to the bed. He'd thrown the pills on the bedside chest, and he took two and opened the top drawer to put them in.

And there it was.

Lying in the drawer, jumbled up with pens and cufflinks and bits of loose change. Oh, Lord. Slowly, almost reluctantly, he pulled the little frame out and stared down at the faces laughing back up at him—Rachel, full of life as usual, sitting on the grass with Ben in between her knees, his little hands filled with grass mowings and his eyes alight with mischief. He'd been throwing the grass mowings all over her, and they'd all been laughing.

And six months later, five years ago today, they'd been mown down by a drunk driver who'd just left his office Christmas party. They'd been doing some last-minute shopping—collecting a watch she'd bought him, he discovered when he eventually went through the bag of their things he'd been given at the hospital. He'd worn it every day for the last five years—until it had been shattered, smashed to bits against an alpine tree during the avalanche.

An avalanche that had brought him home—to a woman called Amelia, and her three innocent and displaced children.

Was this Rachel's doing? Trying to tell him to move on, to forget them both?

He traced their faces with his finger, swallowing down the grief that had never really left him, the grief that sent him away every Christmas to try and forget the unforgettable, to escape the inescapable.

He put the photo back in the drawer and closed it softly, turned off the light, then lay back down and stared dry-eyed into the night.

She couldn't sleep.

Something had woken her—some strange sound, although how she could know the sounds of the house so well already she had no idea, but somehow she did, and this one was strange.

She got out of bed and checked the children, but all of them were sleeping, Thomas flat out on his back with his arms flung up over his head, Edward on his tummy with one leg stuck out the side, and Kitty curled on her side with her hand under her cheek and her battered old teddy snuggled in the crook of her arm.

So not them, then.

Jake?

She looked over the banisters, but all was quiet and there was no light.

Rufus?

Oh, Lord, Rufus. Did he want to go out? Was that what had woken her, him yipping or scratching at the door?

She pulled on a jumper over her pyjamas—because, of course, in her haste she'd left her dressing gown on the back of the door at her sister's—and tiptoed down the stairs, glancing along to Jake's room as she reached the head of the lower flight.

She'd brought his luggage up earlier while he was sleeping and put it in there, because he couldn't possibly manage to lug it up there himself, and she'd had her first look at his room.

It was over the formal drawing room, with an arched opening to the bathroom at the bay window end, and a great rolltop bath sat in the middle, with what must be the most spectacular view along the endless lawn to the woods in the distance. She couldn't picture him in it at all, there was a huge double shower the size of the average wetroom that seemed much more likely, and a pair of gleaming washbasins, and in a separate little room with its own basin and marble-tiled walls was a loo.

And at the opposite end of the room was the bed. Old, solid, a vast and imposing four-poster, the head end and the top filled in with heavily carved panelling, it was perfect for the room. Perfect for the house. The sort of bed where love was made and children were born and people slipped quietly away at the end of their lives, safe in its arms.

It was a wonderful, wonderful bed. And not in the least monastic. She could picture him in it so easily.

Was he lying in it now? She didn't know. Maybe, maybe not—and she was mad to think about it.

There was no light on, and the house was in silence, but it felt different, she thought. There was something about it which had changed with his arrival, a sort of—rightness, as if the house had relaxed now he was home.

Which didn't explain what had woken her. And the door to his room was open a crack. She'd gone down to let the dog out and tidy up the kitchen after she'd settled the children and finished unpacking their things and he must have come upstairs by then, but she hadn't noticed the door open. Perhaps he'd come out again to get something and hadn't shut it, and that was what had woken her, but there was no sign of him now.

She went down to the breakfast room, guided only by the moonlight, and opened the door, and she heard the gentle thump of the dog's tail on the floor and the clatter of his nails.

'Hello, my lovely man,' she crooned, crouching down and pulling gently on his ears. 'Are you all right?'

'I take it you're talking to the dog.'

She gave a little shriek and pressed her hand to her chest, then started to laugh. 'Good grief, Jake, you scared me to death!' She straightened up and reached for the light, then hesitated, conscious of her tired old pyjamas. 'Are you OK?'

'I couldn't sleep. You?'

'I thought I heard a noise.'

He laughed softly. 'In this house? Of course you heard a noise! It creaks like a ship.'

'I know. It settles. I love it—it sounds as if it's relaxing. No, there was something else. It must have been you.'

'I stumbled over the dog—he came to see me and I hadn't put the light on and I kicked him by accident and he yelped—and, before you ask, he's fine. I nudged him, really, but he seemed a bit upset by it, so I sat with him.'

'Oh, I'm so sorry—he does get underfoot and—well, I think he was kicked as a puppy. Has he forgiven you?'

The soft sound of Jake's laughter curled round her again, warming her. 'I think so. He's been on my lap.'

'Ah. Sounds like it, then.' She hesitated, wondering if she should leave him to it and go back to bed, but sensing that there was something wrong, something more than he was telling her. 'How's the fire?'

'OK. I think it could do with more wood.'

'I'll get some.'

She went out of the back door and brought in an armful of logs, putting on the kitchen light as she went, and she left it on when she came back, enough to see by but hopefully not enough to see just how tired her pyjamas really were, and the spill of yellow light made the room seem cosy and intimate.

Which was absurd, considering its size, but everything was in scale and so it didn't seem big, just—safe.

She put the logs in the basket and opened the fire, throwing some in, and as the flames leapt up she went to shut it but he stopped her.

'Leave it open. It's nice to sit and stare into the flames. It helps—'

Helps? Helps what? she wanted to ask, but she couldn't, somehow, so she knelt there on the hearthrug in the warmth of the flames, with Rufus snuggled against her side, his skinny, feathery tail wafting against her, and waited.

But Jake didn't say any more, just sighed and dropped his head back against the chair and closed his eyes. She could see that his fingers were curled around a glass, and on the table behind him was a bottle. The whisky?

'What?'

She jumped guiltily. 'Nothing.'

He snorted. 'It's never nothing with women. Yes, it's the whisky. No, it doesn't help.'

'Jake—'

'No. Leave it, Amelia. Please. If you want to do something useful, you could make us a cup of tea.'

'How about a hot milky drink?'

'I'm not five.'

'No, but you're tired, you're hurt and you said you'd had enough caffeine today—it might help you sleep.'

'Tea,' he said implacably.

She shrugged and got to her feet, padded back through to the kitchen and put the kettle on, turning in time to see him drain his glass and set it down on the table. He glanced up and met her eyes, and sighed.

'I've only had one. I'm not an alcoholic, Amelia.'

'I never suggested you were!' she said, appalled that he'd think she was criticising when actually she'd simply been concerned for his health and well-being.

'So stop looking at me as if you're the Archangel Gabriel and I'm going off the rails!'

She gave a soft chuckle and took two mugs out of the cupboard. 'I'm the last person to criticise anyone for life choices. I'm homeless, for heavens' sake! And I've got three children, only one of whom was planned, and I'm unemployed and my life's a total mess, so pardon me if I pick you up on that one! I just wondered…'

'Wondered what? Why I'm such a miserable bastard?'

'Are you? Miserable, I mean? Kate thought—' She broke off, not wanting him to think Kate had been discussing him, but it was too late, and one eyebrow climbed autocratically.

'Kate thought—?' he prompted.

'You were just a loner. You are, I mean. A loner.'

'And what do you think, little Miss Fixit?'

She swallowed. 'I think you're sad, and lonely. She said you're very private, but I think that's because it all hurts too much to talk about.'

His face lost all expression, and he turned back to the fire, the only sign of movement from him the flex of the muscle in his jaw. 'Why don't you forget the amateur psychology and concentrate on making the tea?' he said, his voice devoid of emotion, but she could still see that tic in his jaw, the rhythmic bunching of the muscle, and she didn't know whether to persevere or give up, because she sensed it might all be a bit of a Pandora's box and, once opened, she might well regret all the things that came out.

So she made the tea, and took it through and sat beside the fire in what started as a stiff and unyielding silence and became in the end a wary truce.

He was the first to break the silence.

'I don't suppose you've made the shopping list?'

She shook her head. 'Not yet. I could do it now.'

'No, don't worry. We can do it over breakfast. I have no doubt that, no matter how little sleep we may have had, the kids will be up at the crack of dawn raring to go, so there'll be plenty of time.'

She laughed a little unsteadily, feeling the tension drain out of her at his words. 'I'm sure.' She got to her feet and held out her hand for his mug, then was surprised when he reached up his left hand, the one in the cast, and took her fingers in his.

'Ignore me, Amelia. I'll get over it. I'll be fine tomorrow.'

She nodded, not understanding really, because how could she? But she let it go, for now at least, and she squeezed his fingers gently and then let go, and he dropped his arm and held out the mug.

'Thanks for the tea. It was nice.'

The tea? Or having someone to sit and drink it with?

He didn't say, and she wasn't asking, but one thing she knew about this man, whatever Kate might say to the contrary—he wasn't a loner.

'My pleasure,' she murmured and, putting the mugs in the sink, she closed the doors of the fire and shut it down again. With a murmured, 'Good night,' she went upstairs to bed, but she didn't sleep until she heard the soft creak of the stairs and the little click as his bedroom door closed.

Then she let out the breath she'd been holding and slipped into a troubled and uneasy sleep.

CHAPTER FIVE

IT WAS the first time in years he'd been round a supermarket, and Christmas Eve probably wasn't the day to start—not when they even had to queue to get into the car park, and by the time they'd found a space Jake was beginning to wonder why on earth he'd suggested it.

It was going to be a nightmare, he knew it, rammed to the roof with festive goodies and wall-to-wall Christmas jingles and people in silly hats—he was dreading it, and it didn't disappoint.

The infuriatingly jolly little tunes on the in-store speakers were constantly being interrupted with calls for multi-skilled staff to go to the checkouts—a fact that didn't inspire hope for a quick getaway—and the place was rammed with frustrated shoppers who couldn't reach the shelves for the trolleys jamming the aisles.

'I have an idea,' he said as they fought to get down the dairy aisle and he was shunted in the ankle by yet another trolley. 'You know what we need, I don't want to be shoved around and Thomas needs company, so why don't I stand at the end with him and you go backwards and forwards picking up the stuff?'

And it all, suddenly, got much easier because he could concentrate on amusing Thomas—and that actually was probably the hardest part. Not that he was hard to entertain, quite the opposite, but it brought back so many memories—memories he'd buried with his son—and it was threatening to wreck him. Then, just when he thought he'd go mad if he had to look at that cheerful, chubby little smile any longer, he realised their system wasn't working.

The trolley wasn't getting fuller and, watching her, he could see why. She was obviously reluctant to spend too much of his money, which was refreshing but unnecessary, so he gave up and shoved the trolley one-handed into the fray while she was dithering over the fresh turkeys.

'What's the matter?'

'They're so expensive. The frozen ones are much cheaper—'

'But they take ages to defrost so we don't have a choice. Just pick one. Here, they've got nice free-range Bronze turkeys—get one of them,' he suggested, earning himself a searching look.

'What do you know about Bronze turkeys?' she asked incredulously.

He chuckled. 'Very little—but I know they're supposed to have the best flavour, I'm ethically comfortable with free range and, anyway, they're the most expensive and therefore probably the most sought after. That's usually an indicator of quality. So pick one and let's get on.'

'But—they're so expensive, Jake, and I feel so guilty taking your money—'

He gave up, reached over and single-handedly heaved a nice fat turkey into the trolley. 'Right. Next?'

'Um—stuffing,' she said weakly, and he felt a little tug at his sleeve.

'You said we could have sausages and cook them and have them on sticks,' Kitty said hopefully.

'Here—traditional chipolatas,' he said, and threw three packets in the trolley, thought better of it and added another two for good measure. 'Bacon?'

'Um—probably.' She put a packet of sausagemeat stuffing in the trolley and he frowned at it, picked up another with chestnuts and cranberries, which looked more interesting, and put that in, too.

'You're getting into this, aren't you?' she teased, coming back with the bacon.

So was she, he noticed with relief, seeing that at last she was picking up the quality products and not the cheapest, smallest packet she could find of whatever it was. They moved on, and the trolley filled up. Vegetables, fruit, a traditional Christmas pudding that would last them days, probably, but would at least be visible in the middle of the old refectory table in the breakfast room, and a chocolate log for the children. Then, when they'd done the food shopping and filled the trolley almost to the brim, they took it through the checkout, put it all in the car and went back inside for 'the exciting stuff', as Kitty put it.

Christmas decorations for the tree they had yet to buy, little nets of chocolate coins in gold foil, crackers for the table, a wreath for the door—the list was nearly as long as the first and, by the time they got to the end of it, the children were hungry and Thomas, who'd been as good as gold and utterly, heart-wrenchingly enchanting until that point, was starting to grizzle.

'I tell you what—why don't you take the kids and get them something to eat and drink while I deal with this lot?' he suggested, peeling a twenty pound note out of his wallet and giving it to her.

She hesitated, but he just sighed and shoved it at her, and with a silent nod she flashed him a smile and took the children off to the canteen.

Which gave him long enough to go back up the aisles and look for presents for them all. And, because it had thinned out by that point, he went to the customer services and asked if there was anyone who could help him wrap the presents for the children. He brandished his cast pathetically and, between that and the black eye, he charmed them into it shamelessly.

There was nothing outrageous in his choices. There was nothing outrageous in the shop anyway but, even if there had been, he would have avoided it. It wasn't necessary, and he didn't believe in spoiling children, but there was a colouring book with glue and glitter that Kitty had fingered longingly and been made to put back, and he'd noticed Edward looking at an intricate construction toy of the sort he'd loved as a boy, and there was a nice chunky plastic shape sorter which he thought Thomas might like.

And then there was Amelia.

She didn't have any gloves, he'd noticed, and he'd commented on it on the way there when she was rubbing her hands and blowing on them holding the steering wheel.

'Sure, it's freezing, but I can't do things with gloves on,' she'd explained.

But he'd noticed some fingerless mitts, with little flaps that buttoned back out of the way and could be let down to tuck her fingers into to turn them into mittens. And they were in wonderful, ludicrously pink stripes with a matching scarf that would snuggle round her neck and keep her warm while she walked the dog.

He even bought a little coat for Rufus, because he'd noticed him shivering out on their walk first thing.

And then he had to make himself stop, because they weren't his family and he didn't want to make them—or, more specifically, Amelia—feel embarrassed. But he chucked in a jigsaw to put on the low coffee table in the drawing room and work on together, just because it was the sort of thing he'd loved in his childhood, and also a family game they could play together.

And then he really *did* stop, and they were all wrapped and paid for, together with the decorations, and someone even helped him load them into the car and wished him a merry Christmas, and he found himself saying it back with a smile.

Really?

He went into the canteen and found them sitting in a litter of sandwich wrappers and empty cups. 'All set?'

She nodded. 'Yes. We were just coming to find you. Thank you so much—'

'Don't mention it. Right, we'd better get on, because we need to take this lot home and then get a tree before it's too late, and at some point today I need to go to the hospital and have a proper cast put on my arm.'

'Wow! Look at the tree. It's *enormous*!'

It wasn't, not really, but it was quite big enough—and it had been a bit of a struggle to get it in place with one arm out of action in its new cast, but just the look on the children's faces made it all worth it—and, if he wasn't mistaken, there was the sheen of tears in Amelia's eyes.

They'd put it in pride of place in the bay window in the drawing room, and lit the fire—a great roaring log fire in the open hearth, with crackling flames and the sweet smell of apple-wood smoke—and, between the wood smoke and the heady scent of the tree, the air just smelled of Christmas. All they had to do now was decorate the tree, and for Jake it was a step too far.

'I'm going to sit this out,' he said, heading for the door, but Kitty shook her head and grabbed his good hand and tugged him back, shocking him into immobility.

'You *can't*, Jake! You have to help us—we're all too small to reach the top, and you *have* to put the *lights* on and the *fairy* and all the tinsel and *everything*!'

Why was it, he wondered, that children—especially earnest little girls—always talked in italics and exclamation marks? And her eyes were pleading with him, and there was no way he could walk away from her. From any of them.

'OK. I'll just go and put the kettle on—'

'No! Lights first, because otherwise we can't do *anything* until you get back, and you'll be *ages*!'

Italics again. He smiled at her. 'Well, in that case, I'll put the *lights* on *first*, but *just* the lights, and then we'll have a *quick* cup of tea and we'll finish it off. OK?'

She eyed him a little suspiciously, as if she didn't trust his notion of quick and wasn't quite sure about the emphasis on the words, because there was something mildly teasing in them and he could see she was working it out, working out if he *was* only teasing or if he was being mean.

And he couldn't be mean to her, he discovered. Not in the least. In fact, all he wanted to do was gather her up into his arms and tell her it would all be all right, but of course it wasn't his place to do that and he couldn't make it right for her, couldn't make her father step up to the plate and behave like a decent human being.

If he was the man he was thinking of, Jake knew David Jones, had met him in the past, and he hadn't liked him at all. Oh, he'd been charming enough, but he'd talked rubbish, been full of bull and wild ideas with no foundation, and at one point a year or two ago he'd approached him at a conference asking for his investment in some madcap scheme. He'd declined, and he'd heard later, not unexpectedly, that he'd gone down the pan. And it didn't surprise him in the least, if it *was* the same David Jones, that he'd walked out on his family.

So he couldn't make it right for David's little daughter. But he could help her with the tree, and he could make sure they were warm and safely housed until their situation improved. And it was all he needed to do, all his conscience required.

It was only his heart that he was having trouble with, and he shut the door on it firmly and concentrated on getting the lights on the tree without either knocking it over or hurting any more of the innumerable aches and pains that were emerging with every hour that passed.

'Are you OK doing that?'

He turned his head and smiled down at Amelia ruefully. 'I'll live. I'm nearly done.'

'I'll put the kettle on. You look as if you could do with some more painkillers.'

'I'll be fine. It's just stretching that hurts—'

'And bending over, and standing, and—'

'Just put the kettle on,' he said softly, and she opened her mouth again, closed it and went out.

He watched her walk down the hall, watched the gentle sway of her hips, the fluid grace of her movements, the lightness in her step that hadn't been there yesterday, and he felt a sharp stab of what could only be lust. She was a beautiful, sensuous woman, intelligent and brave, and he realised he wanted to gather her up in his arms, too, and to hell with the complications.

But he couldn't, and he wouldn't, so with a quiet sigh he turned back to the tree and finished draping the string of lights around the bottom, then turned them on and stood back.

'How's that?'

'*Really* pretty!' Kitty whispered, awed.

'It's a bit crooked,' he said, wondering if there was any way he could struggle in under the tree and right it, but Edward—typically—rushed in with reassurance.

'It doesn't show,' he said quickly, 'and it looks really nice. Can we put the rest of the things on now?'

'We have to wait for Mummy!' Kitty said, sounding appalled, and so Jake sent them off to the kitchen to find out what she was doing and to tell her to bring biscuits with the tea. He lowered himself carefully on to the sofa and smiled at Thomas, who was sitting on the floor inside a ring of fat cushions with a colourful plastic teething ring in his mouth.

'All right, little man?' he asked, and Thomas gave him a toothy grin and held out the toy. It was covered in spit, but it didn't matter, he was only showing it to Jake, not offering it to him, so he admired it dutifully and tried oh, so hard not to think about Ben.

'That's really nice,' he said gruffly. 'Does it taste good?'

'Mumum,' he said, shoving it back in his mouth with a delicious chuckle, and Jake clenched his teeth and gave a tiny huff of laughter that was more than halfway to a sob.

What was it about kids that they got through your defences like nothing else on earth?

'You're going to be a proper little charmer, aren't you?' he said softly, and was rewarded with another spitty little chuckle. Then he threw down the toy and held out his hands, and it was beyond Jake to refuse.

He held out his hands, hoping his broken wrist was up to it, and Thomas grabbed his fingers and pulled himself up with a delighted gurgle, taking Jake's breath away.

'Are you all right?'

'Not really,' he said a little tightly, massively relieved to see Amelia reappear. 'Um—could you take him? My hand—'

'Oh, Jake! Thomas, come here, darling.'

She gently prised his fingers off Jake's, and the pull on the fracture eased and he sank back with a shaky sigh, because it hadn't only been the fracture, it had been that gummy, dribbly smile and the feel of those strong, chubby little fingers, and he just wanted to get the hell out. 'Thanks. That was probably a stupid thing to do, but—'

'You couldn't refuse him? Tell me about it. Look, I've brought you something lovely!'

'I don't really want a cup of juice,' he said softly, and she laughed, the sound running through him like a tinkling stream, clean and pure and sweet.

'Silly. Your tea's there, with the painkillers.'

He found a smile. Actually, not that hard, with the warmth of her laughter still echoing through him. 'Thanks.'

'And chocolate biscuits, and shortbread!' Edward said, sounding slightly amazed.

'Goodness. Anyone would think it was Christmas,' he said in mock surprise, and Kitty giggled and then, before he could react or do anything to prevent it, she climbed onto his lap and snuggled up against his chest with a smile.

'It *is* Christmas, silly—well, it is tomorrow,' she corrected, and squirmed round to study the tree. 'We need to put everything else on it.'

'Biscuits first,' he said firmly, because he needed his painkillers, especially if Kitty was going to bounce and fidget and squirm on his bruises. And his arm was really aching now after all the silly things he'd done with it that day.

So they ate biscuits, and Kitty snuggled closer, and he caught the anguished look in Amelia's eye and felt so sad for them all that it had all gone wrong, because Kitty's father should have been sitting somewhere else with her on his lap instead of hiding from his responsibilities in Thailand, and he should have been there with Rachel and Ben, and none of them had deserved it—

'Right. Let's do the tree,' he said and, shunting Kitty off his lap, he got stiffly to his feet and put the baubles where he was told.

* * *

He was being amazing.

She couldn't believe just how kind he'd been all day. He'd been so foul to her yesterday, so sarcastic and bitter, but somehow all that was gone and he was being the man Kate had talked about, generous to a fault and the soul of kindness.

He was so gentle with the children, teasing them, humouring them, putting up with their enthusiastic nonsense, and then, when the tree was done and she'd swept underneath it to pick up the needles that had fallen out of it while they'd decorated it, they went into the kitchen and she cooked supper while she danced around the kitchen with tinsel in her hair, singing along with the Christmas songs on the radio and making Thomas giggle.

And then she'd looked up and seen Jake watching her with an odd look on his face, and she'd felt the breath squeeze out of her lungs. No. She was misreading the signals. He couldn't possibly want her—not a destitute woman with three children and a smelly, expensive little dog.

So she pulled the tinsel out of her hair and tied it round the dog's neck, and concentrated on cooking the supper.

Sausages on sticks for Kitty, with roasted vegetable skewers in mini pitta pockets so she could pretend she was having kebabs, followed by the sort of fruit Millie couldn't afford to buy, cut into cubes and dunked into melted chocolate. He'd put little pots on the top of the Aga with squares of chocolate in, and they'd melted and made the most fabulous sauce.

And the children had loved every mouthful of it. Even Thomas had sucked on a bit of sausage and had a few slices of banana and some peeled grapes dipped in chocolate and, apart from the shocking mess, it was a huge success.

'Right, you lot, time for bed,' she said.

'Oh, but it's Christmas!'

'Yes, and it'll come all the earlier if you're in bed asleep,' she reasoned. 'And Father Christmas won't come down the chimney if you're still awake.'

'But he won't come anyway, because of the fire,' Kitty said, looking suddenly worried, but Jake rescued the situation instantly.

'Not a problem,' he said promptly. 'There's another chimney in the dining room, and he'll come down that.'

'But he won't know where to put the presents!' she argued.

'Yes, he will, because he knows everything,' Edward said with an air of patient indulgence that made Millie want to laugh and cry all at once. 'Come on, let's go up to bed and then he'll come.'

'Promise?' Kitty said, staring at her hopefully.

Oh, Lord, there was so little for them. They were going to be horribly disappointed. 'Promise,' she said, near to tears, but then the doorbell rang, jangling the ancient bell over the breakfast room door, and Jake got to his feet.

'I'll get it, it's probably Kate,' he said, and she followed him, meaning to say hello if it *was* Kate or take the children up to bed if not, but as he reached for the door they heard the unmistakable sound of a choir.

'Carol singers,' he said in a hollow voice, rooted to the spot with an appalled expression on his face.

'I'll deal with them,' she said softly, and opened the door, meaning to give them some change for their tin and send them away. But he was still standing there in full view and the vicar, who was standing at the front, beamed at him.

'Mr Forrester! We heard you were back and that you'd been injured, so we thought we'd come and share some carols with you on the way back from evensong—bring you a little Christmas cheer.'

Jake opened his mouth, shut it again and smiled a little tightly. 'Thank you,' he said, and he probably would have stood there with that frozen smile on his face if Amelia hadn't elbowed him gently out of the way, opened the door wide and invited them in, because after all there was no choice, no matter how unhappy it might make him.

'You'll freeze,' she said with a smile. 'Come inside and join us.' And Jake would just have to cope, because anything else would have been too rude for words. And apparently he realised that, because he found another smile and stepped back.

'Yes—of course, come on in by the fire,' he said, and led them to the drawing room, where they gathered round the fire and sang all the old favourites—*Silent Night*, *Away In A Manger* and *O Come All Ye Faithful*, and then the vicar smilingly apologised for not having a chorister to sing *Once In Royal David's City*, and beside her Amelia felt Edward jiggle and she squeezed his shoulder in encouragement.

'Go on,' she murmured, and he took a step forwards.

'I could do it,' he offered, and the vicar looked at him and smiled broadly.

'Well—please do. Do you need the words?'

He shook his head, went over to them and started to sing.

Jake was speechless.

The boy's voice filled the room, pure and sweet, and he felt his throat close. It brought so much back—the pain of his childhood, the respite that music had brought him, the hard work but the immense rewards of being a chorister.

And when Edward got to the end of the first verse and everyone joined in, he found himself singing, too, found the voice he'd grown into as a man, rusty with lack of use and emotion, but warming up, filling him with joy again as he sang the familiar carol. And Edward looked at him in astonishment and then smiled, as if he'd just discovered something wonderful.

And maybe he had.

Maybe Jake had, too, because Edward had a truly beautiful voice and it would be a travesty if he didn't get the opportunity to develop and explore this musical gift. And if there was anything he could do to help with that, he wanted to do it, even if it was just to encourage him to join the school choir.

But in the meantime he sang, and the choir launched into *God Rest Ye Merry Gentlemen*, which was perfect for his baritone, and so for the first time in years he dragged the air deep down into his lungs and let himself go, and the old house was filled with the joyful sound of their voices.

And Edward grinned, and he grinned back, and beside him he could see Amelia staring up at him in astonishment, her eyes like saucers, and Kitty too. When they got to the end they all smiled and laughed, and Amelia ran down to the kitchen and came back with a tray of mince pies she'd made earlier, and he offered them a drink to wash them down but they all refused.

'Sorry, we'd love to, but we have to get home,' was the consensus, and of course they did. It was Christmas Eve, and he'd been fitted in as a favour. A favour by people he didn't know, who'd heard he'd been hurt and had come to bring Christmas to him, and deep down inside, the fissure that was opening around his heart cracked open a little further, letting the warmth seep in.

'Thank you so much for coming,' he said with genuine feeling as he showed them out. 'The children have really enjoyed it. It was extremely kind of you, and I can't thank you enough.'

'Well, there's always the church roof,' the vicar joked, and he laughed, but he made a mental note to send him a cheque. 'And if the boy wants to join us…'

'Ah, they're only visiting,' he said, and the words gave him a curious pang, as if somehow that was wrong and vaguely unsettling. 'But—yes, I agree. He could be a chorister.'

'As you were once, I would imagine. You could always join us yourself. The choir's always got room for a good voice.'

He smiled a little crookedly. 'My choir days are over—but thank you. Have a good Christmas, all of you. Good night.'

They left in a chorus of good-nights and merry Christmases, and he closed the door and turned to see Edward standing there staring at him.

'Did you really sing in a choir?' he asked warily, and Jake nodded.

'Yes, I did. When I was about your age, and a little older. My voice started to break when I was twelve, which rather put a stop to singing for a couple of years, and I never really got back into it after that, but—yeah, I went to choir school. What about you? Do you sing in a choir?'

'We didn't really have a choir at the school, but the music teacher said I ought to have a voice test somewhere. I was supposed to sing in the school carol concert last week, but we had to move to Auntie Laura's and it was too far away, so I couldn't. And I'd been practising for weeks and weeks.'

'I can tell. What a shame. Still, you did it for us, and it was great. You did really well. Here, come with me. I've got something to show you.'

'Is it a picture?'

'No. It's a film of me when I was in the choir. I had to sing *Once In Royal David's City* myself at the start of the carol service when I was twelve, just before my voice broke.'

And it had been televised, but he didn't mention that because it was irrelevant, really. He took Edward into his sitting room, found the DVD he'd had the old video copied onto, and turned it on.

'Wow,' Edward said at the end of his solo, his voice hushed. 'That was amazing. You must have been so scared.'

He laughed. 'I was pretty terrified, I can tell you. But it was worth it, it was fantastic. It was a good time all round. Hard work, but lots of fun, too, and I wouldn't have swapped it for the world.'

He told him more about it, about the fun, about the pranks he'd got up to and the trouble he'd got in, and about the hard work and the gruelling schedule of rehearsals, but also about the amazing thrill and privilege of singing in the cathedral.

'I'd love to do that,' the boy said wistfully.

'Would you? It's a big commitment. I had to go to boarding school, but then I wasn't very happy at home, so actually I enjoyed it,' he found himself admitting.

'Why weren't you happy?' Edward asked.

'Oh—my parents used to row a lot, and I always seemed to be in the way. So it was quite nice when I wasn't, for all of us, really. But you are happy, aren't you?'

He nodded. 'And I couldn't leave Mummy, because she needs me.'

'Of course she does—but, you know, she also needs you to be happy, and if it made you happy—anyway, you don't have to go away to school. Most schools have a choir, and certainly the bigger churches do. I'm sure they'd be delighted to have you. You've got a good voice.'

'But we don't live anywhere properly, so we don't have a church or a school,' he said, and Jake's heart ached for the poor, uprooted child.

'You will soon,' he consoled him, hoping it was true, and he turned off the television and got to his feet. 'Now, you'd better run up to bed or I'm going to be in trouble with your mother. You sleep well, and I'll see you in the morning. Good night, Edward.'

'Good night,' Edward said, and then without warning he ran over to Jake, put his arms round him and hugged him before running out of the door. And Jake stood there, rooted to the spot, unravelled by the simple spontaneous gesture of a child.

Amelia stood in the shadows of the hall, scarcely able to breathe for emotion.

The sound of his voice had been exquisite, the sort of sound that made your hair stand on end and your heart swell, and she'd stood there and listened to it, then to his gentle and revealing conversation with her son, and her eyes had filled with tears. Poor little boy, to have felt so unwanted and unloved. And thank God for a choir school which had helped him through it, given him something beautiful and perfect to compensate in some small way for the disappointments of his young life.

She'd taken Kitty and Thomas upstairs when she'd seen Edward deep in conversation with Jake, knowing he missed the influence of a man in his life, and she'd bathed them quickly, tucked them up and gone back down—and heard the pure, sweet sound of a chorister coming from Jake's sitting room.

She hadn't known it was him until she'd heard him talking to Edward, but she wasn't surprised. It had been obvious when he'd joined in with the carol singers that he'd had some kind of voice training, as well as a beautiful voice, deep and rich and warm. It had shivered through her then, and it had done the same thing now, hearing him as a child.

And he was talking to Edward about it, treating him as an equal, encouraging him, giving him hope—

But too much hope, and it was pointless doing that,

because there was no way she could afford any lessons or anything for him, so it was cruel of Jake to encourage him. It was easy if you had money. Everything was easier, and it wasn't fair to Edward to build him up. She'd have to talk to Jake, to stop him—

She dived into the kitchen and scrubbed the tears away from her eyes while she cleared up the aftermath of their supper, and then she took the presents she'd brought downstairs with her through to the drawing room—the few things she'd bought the children, and the ones from Kate, and of course the beautiful and inevitably expensive ones from her sister—and, by the time she got there, there were some others waiting.

They must be Jake's, she thought. Presents from friends, if not family, and people like Kate, who was bound to have given him a present.

But they weren't. They were for the children, and for her, and, of all things, for Rufus. Her eyes flooded with tears, and she sat back on her heels and sniffed.

Damn him, how could he do this? Squandering money on them all because it was so easy for him, not realising how much worse it made it all, how much harder it would be when it was all over and they came down to earth with a bump. He was even spoiling the wretched dog—

'Amelia?'

'What are these? You shouldn't—' she began, but he just shook his head.

'They're nothing—'

'No. They're not nothing,' she corrected tautly. 'They're nothing to you, but believe me, you have no idea what nothing's like. Nothing is not having anywhere for your

children to live, having to take them away from school just
before the carol concert your son's been practising for for
weeks, having to tell them that Daddy doesn't have any
money and he's not even here to see them because he's run
away from the law—except of course I can't tell them that,
can I, because it wouldn't be fair, so I have to pretend he's
just had to go away and lie to them, and I'm sick of lying
to them and struggling and the last—absolutely the *last*
damn thing I need is you telling Edward he should go to
choir school. I'll never be able to afford it and you'll just
build his hopes up and then they'll be dashed and it's just
another disappointment in his life—'

She couldn't go on, tears streaming down her cheeks,
and he gave a ragged sigh and crouched awkwardly down
beside her, his hand gentle on her shoulder, his eyes dis-
tressed. 'Amelia—Millie—please don't,' he murmured
softly. 'It wasn't like that. I didn't build his hopes up, but
he's good, and there are places—'

'Didn't you *hear* what I said?' she raged. '*We have no
money!*'

'But you don't need money. He could get a scholarship, like I did. My parents didn't pay. If someone's got
talent, they don't turn them away—and there are other
things. It doesn't have to be choir school. Just because I
went there doesn't mean it's right for everyone. It's very
hard, and the hours are really long, and you work every
Sunday, Christmas Day, Easter—you have to be dedicated, it's a massive commitment, and it's not for everybody—'

'No, it's not, but even if it was for him, it's not for you
to decide! He's my son, Jake—*mine*! It's none of your

business! You have no right to take him off like that and fill his head with ideas—'

'It wasn't like that! He was asking…I just thought…'

'Well, don't! If you want a son to follow in your footsteps, then get your own, Jake, but leave mine out of it! And we don't need your flashy presents!'

And, without giving him a chance to reply, she scrambled to her feet and ran into the kitchen, tears pouring down her face and furious with herself as well as him because, whatever he'd done, whatever he'd spent or said, they were in his house against his wishes, and he'd busted a gut today to make their Christmas Day tomorrow a good one, and now she'd gone and ruined it for all of them…

CHAPTER SIX

IF YOU want a son…

His legs gave way and he sat down abruptly on the rug in front of the tree, her words ringing in his ears.

It had never occurred to him he was doing any harm by talking to Edward, showing him the recording. He was just sharing an interest, taking an interest—and not because he wanted a son to follow in his footsteps. He'd been there, done that, and lost everything. She thought he didn't know what nothing meant? Well, he had news for her.

Nothing meant waking up every morning alone, with nobody to share your day with, nobody to help you live out your dreams, nobody to love, nobody to love you in return.

Nothing meant standing in a cold and lonely churchyard staring at a headstone bearing the names of the only people in the world you cared about and wondering how on earth it had happened, how one minute they'd been there, and the next they'd been gone for ever.

If you want a son…

Pain seared through him. *Oh, Ben, I want you. I want you every day. What would you have been like? Would you have loved singing, like me, or would you have been tone-deaf like your mother? Tall or short? Quiet or noisy? I would have loved you, whatever. I'll always love you.* He glanced out of the window and saw a pale swirl of snow, and his heart contracted. *Are you cold tonight, my precious son, lying there in the churchyard?*

Oh, God.

A sob ripped through him and he stifled it, battening it down, refusing to allow it to surface. She hadn't meant to hurt him. She hadn't known about Ben, hadn't realised what she was saying. And maybe she was right. Maybe he'd overstepped the mark with Edward.

He needed to talk to her, to go and find her and apologise—but not yet. Not now. Now, he needed to get himself under control, to let the pain recede a little.

And then he became aware of Rufus, standing just a few inches away from him, his tail down, his eyes worried, and when he held out his hand, the dog's tail flickered briefly.

'Oh, Rufus. What's happened to us all?' he murmured unsteadily, and Rufus came and sat down with his side against Jake's thigh, and rested his head in his lap and licked his hand.

'Yeah, I know. I need to talk to Amelia. I need to tell her I'm sorry. But I can't—'

He bit his lip, and Rufus licked him again, and he ruffled his fur and waited a little longer, until his emotions were back under control, because he owed Amelia more than just an apology. He owed her an explanation, and it would mean opening himself to her, to her pity, and he never ever did that. It was just too damned hard.

But eventually he couldn't leave it any longer, so he got

stiffly to his feet, found the whisky and limped down the hall to the breakfast room and pushed open the door.

She was sitting in front of the fire, her legs drawn up and her arms wrapped round her knees, and he could tell she'd been crying. Her face was ravaged with tears, her eyes wide with distress. He went over to her, poured two hefty measures of spirit and held one out to her.

'I'm sorry,' he said. 'I should have thought—should have asked you before showing it to him.'

'No. You were only being kind. I was so rude—'

'Yes, you were, but I'm not surprised, with everything going on in your life. You're just fighting their corner. I can't criticise you for that.'

And then, before his courage failed him and he chickened out, he said, 'I had a son.'

She lifted her head and stared at him.

'Had?' she whispered in horrified disbelief.

'Ben. He died five years ago—five years yesterday, just a month after his second birthday. He'd been Christmas shopping with my wife, Rachel, and they were by the entrance to the car park when someone mounted the kerb and hit them. They were both killed instantly.'

'Oh, Jake—'

Her voice was hardly more than a breath, and then she dragged in a shuddering sob and pressed her hand against her lips. Dear God, what had she said to him? If you want a son…then get your own. And all the time—

'Oh, Jake, I don't know what to say—'

'Don't say anything. There's nothing you can say. Here, have a drink. And please don't worry about the presents, they really are nothing. It was just a gesture, nothing more. They aren't lavish, I promise, so you don't have to worry. I wouldn't do that to you. I just…it's Christmas, and I'd expect to give something small to any child who was staying here. And I promise not to say anything more to any of them that might give you a problem later on. So come on, drink up and let's go and stuff the turkey, otherwise we'll be eating at midnight.'

She hauled in a breath, sniffed and scrubbed her cheeks with her hands. 'You're right. We've got a lot to do.' And just then she couldn't talk to him, couldn't say another word or she really would howl her eyes out, and so she sipped the whisky he pressed into her hand, feeling the slow burn as it slid down her throat, letting the warmth drive out the cold horror of his simple words.

No wonder he didn't do children. No wonder he hadn't been pleased to see them in his house, on the very anniversary…

She took a gulp and felt it scorch down her throat. What had it done to him, to come home and find them all there? His words had been cruel, but not as cruel as their presence must have been to him. And her own words—they'd been far more cruel, so infinitely hurtful, and there was nothing she could do to take them back.

'What I said—'

'Don't. Don't go there, Amelia. You weren't to know. Forget it.'

But she couldn't, and she knew she never would. She couldn't bear the thought that she'd hurt him with her words, that their presence in his house must be tearing him apart, but there was nothing she could do about it now—

the words were said, the children were sleeping upstairs, and all she could do was make sure it all went as well and smoothly as possible, and kept the children away from him so they didn't rub salt in his wound.

'I'm going to get on,' she said, and she set the glass down and stood up, brushed herself off mentally and physically, and headed for the kitchen.

'We still haven't dealt with the decorations in here,' he said from behind her, and she looked up at their makeshift decorations in the light fitting over the breakfast table, still half-finished and looking bedraggled and forlorn.

Damn. 'I'm sorry, I meant to take them down,' she said, tugging out a chair, but he just shook his head.

'No. Leave them. The children made them.'

She stopped, one foot on the chair, the other on the table, and looked down at him.

'But—you said it was tat. And you were right, it is.'

'No. I'm sorry. I was just feeling rough and you took me by surprise,' he said, master of the understatement. 'Please, leave them. In fact, weren't there some more bits?'

She nodded and climbed slowly down off the chair. 'Edward put them out of the back door.'

'Get them and put them in—finish it off. And I'll put the wreath we bought on the front door. And then we ought to do the things you need help with, and then I'm really going to have to turn in, because I'm bushed, frankly. It's been a long day, and I've had enough.'

She felt another great wave of guilt. 'Oh, Jake—sit down, let me get you another drink. I can do everything. Please—just sit there and rest and keep me company, if you really want to help, or otherwise just go to bed. I can manage.'

He smiled wryly. 'I'm sure you can. I get the feeling there's not a lot you can't manage. But I'm OK.'

And he helped her, even though he must be feeling pretty rough, because she got the distinct impression that he didn't give up easily. So she made them both a cup of tea, and finished off the decorations in the light fitting while he put the wreath on the door. Then he sat down in the chair to drink his tea while she stuffed the turkey and wrapped the sausages in bacon, and the next time she looked he'd leant back and closed his eyes, with Rufus curled up on his lap and his legs stretched out in front of the fire. She made another batch of mince pies and peeled potatoes and carrots and trimmed the sprouts while they cooked, and then she woke him up and sent him to bed.

It was almost Christmas Day, she thought as she tiptoed into the children's room and hung their stockings on the end of their beds. Nothing like what they'd had last year or the year before, but they were good kids and they under-stood, in their way, and thanks to Jake they had tiny oranges and chocolates and little bits of this and that to add to her offerings.

And at least they were alive, unlike Jake's little boy.

She stared down at Edward. He was a little older than Ben would have been, she realised with a pang. How painful it must be for Jake, knowing that. How could she have said what she did? How did he cope with the terrible loss? How did anyone?

Edward's face blurred, and she kissed him lightly on the cheek, snuggling the quilt up round him, then tucked Kitty in and went to check on Thomas. He didn't have a stocking, but he was only eight months old, he didn't even know what Christmas was yet. And at least he was in a warm, comfortable house.

They were so lucky. They could have been anywhere, and instead they were here, warm and safe—and, without Jake, it would have been so much worse. He'd done so much for them, and she'd repaid him by throwing his kindness back in his face. And not just his kindness.

If you want a son…

Tears scalded her cheeks, and she scrubbed them away. She could never take those words back, but she owed him more than she could ever repay, and she vowed to do everything in her power to make it right.

Starting with giving him a Christmas to remember…

'Mummy—Mummy, it's snowing!'

She opened her eyes a crack, but it was still dark—except for a strange light that filtered through the gap in the curtains.

'Kitty, whatever's the time?' she whispered.

'It's nearly six—Mummy, get up and come and *see*! It's so pretty!'

She let Kitty drag her out of bed and over to the window, and sure enough, the garden was blanketed with snow, thick and crisp and brilliant white, eerie in the moonlight.

Whatever time was it? The last thing she wanted was for the children to disturb Jake in the middle of the night! She peered at her watch anxiously. 'Kitty, it's only half past five!'

'No, it's not, it's after, 'cos I waited! And we've got stockings! Come and see!'

'Is Edward awake?'

'Of course I'm awake,' her sleepy, rumpled son said as he came in. 'She's been whispering at me for hours! Happy Christmas, Mummy,' he added with a smile and went into her arms, hugging her hard.

She bent her head and pressed a kiss to his hair, knowing the time for such liberties was probably numbered and enjoying it while she could, and then she scooped Kitty up and kissed her, too, and carried her back into their bedroom, closing the door to keep the noise down.

She snuggled into Amelia's side for a moment, but then wriggled down and ran to her bed. 'Can we open our stockings now?' she asked excitedly.

'All right,' she agreed reluctantly. 'But just the stockings. Nothing under the tree until later.' Much later!

'Are there presents under the tree? Did you see them?' Kitty asked, wide-eyed and eager, and Millie could have kicked herself for mentioning it.

'I expect there might be,' she said. *Unless there have been burglars.* 'But you can't go down and look until much, much later, in case you disturb Jake.'

And that wasn't going to happen if she had anything to do with it.

'How much later?' Kitty asked, persistent to the last, and she rolled her eyes and laughed softly.

'Half past eight,' she said, 'and that's only if Jake's awake. And if you wake him by making too much noise, then you'll have to wait till ten,' she added, trying to look stern.

'Ten?' Kitty wailed softly, and scrambled onto the bed. 'I'll be very, very quiet,' she vowed. 'Edward, don't make a noise!'

'I haven't said a thing!' he whispered indignantly, climbing onto his own bed and sliding a hand down inside his stocking. 'You're the one making all the noise—'

'Stop that, or the stockings go.'

There was instant silence, broken only by the tiny squeals of excitement from Kitty and the murmured, 'Oh, brilliant!' from Edward when he found a page-a-day diary. He flashed her a huge smile, and she felt a lump in her throat. It was such a little thing, but since David had left he'd kept a diary every day, and she knew he was using it as a way of working through his feelings.

He was such a good kid—and Jake was right, he deserved every chance. She'd look into getting him that voice test, but she was so afraid of tempting fate, of dangling something under his nose and then having it snatched away yet again.

'A chocolate Father Christmas!' Kitty said in delight, delving deeper. 'And a satsuma! Can I eat them now? Pretty please with a cherry on top?'

She sat down with a chuckle on the end of the bed and watched as her children found innocent pleasure in the simplest things. Then Edward looked up with hopeful eyes and said, 'Can we make a snowman?'

It was on the tip of her tongue to say, Of course, when she remembered it wasn't her garden, and she smiled ruefully.

'We'll have to ask Jake,' she said.

Edward nodded and went back to his orange, peeling it

meticulously and savouring it segment by segment. He was so thorough, so methodical in everything he did. So very unlike his father, who rushed into everything without thought. And out of it again. Like marriage. And father-hood.

No, she wasn't going to think about that now. She could hear Thomas starting to stir, and she went back and scooped him out of his cot and gave him a hug. 'Hello, my little man!' she crooned softly. 'Happy Christmas. Look, Thomas—it's snowing!'

And, lifting the curtain aside, she looked out into the garden and saw Jake standing out there with Rufus, racing around in the snow and barking his head off as he tried to bite the snowflakes, while Jake laughed at him.

She chuckled and stood there for a moment watching them. Then, as if his eyes had been drawn to hers, Jake turned and looked up and waved.

She waved back and went in to the children. 'Jake's awake,' she said, 'so I'm going to go down and make a cup of tea and get a bottle for Thomas. Why don't you try and get back to sleep?'

'But we have to say Happy Christmas to Jake!' Kitty said, and ran for the stairs before Amelia could stop her. Edward followed, the two of them thundering and whooping down through the house, and she trailed after them with Thomas, hoping that the onslaught of the children wouldn't prove to be too much for him. Especially now that she knew—

She felt the shadow of his grief fall over the day, and paused a moment to think of a little boy she'd never known and would never have the chance to meet, and the woman who should have been greeting her husband and son here in this house this morning.

'I'm so sorry,' she whispered. 'So, so sorry.'

And then she followed the others downstairs to the kitchen.

It was freezing outside, but there was something wonderful about standing in the snow while Rufus raced round like a puppy and chased the snowflakes.

And as he went back in, the children tumbled into the kitchen, eyes sparkling with excitement, and Kitty ran over to him and reached up. He bent and hugged her, feeling the warm, damp kiss land on his cheek. 'Happy Christmas,' she said, her arms tight around his neck for a second, then she let him go and laughed, and he looked up and met her brother's eyes and remembered last night's spontaneous hug and smiled at him.

'Happy Christmas, Kitty. Happy Christmas, Edward,' he said.

His reply was drowned out by Kitty, plucking at his sleeve and giggling. 'You're all snowy!' she said. 'Like a snowman! Can we make a snowman?'

She was jumping up and down, her enthusiasm infectious, and he grinned down at her. 'Sure. It's great snow for that. It'll stick together. We can do it after we've opened the presents and had breakfast. Well, if that's all right with your mother—'

He looked up and met her eyes, and felt warmth uncurl deep inside him at her smile.

'Of course it's all right. It'll be fun. We can do it whenever you like. But maybe we need to get dressed first.'

'Oh, I don't know, it might be fun for the little cats on your pyjamas to play in the snow,' he teased, and a soft wash of colour swept her cheeks.

'Don't be silly,' she said, a trifle breathlessly, and he felt a totally inappropriate surge of longing.

'Can we make a really huge one?' Edward was asking, and Jake nodded, touched at the grin that blossomed on his usually serious young face.

'The biggest.'

'In the *world*?' Kitty said, her eyes like saucers, and he laughed.

'Well—maybe not *quite*.'

'He'll need a hat.'

'I might have a ski hat he can borrow,' Jake suggested. 'And a scarf.'

'And some coal for his eyes and a carrot for his nose— Mummy, have we got a carrot?'

Amelia threw up her hands and laughed. 'Kitty, slow down! Yes, we've got a carrot. You watched me buy them.'

'Awesome,' she said. 'So can we open the presents now? You said we had to wait till Jake was awake, but he's awake already, so can we go and do it now, and then we can get dressed and go and build our snowman?'

Catching the look on her face, Jake intervened rapidly. 'No, it's too early. Let your mother have a cup of tea and feed the baby. I tell you what,' he went on, watching their faces fall, 'why don't you go and see if you can guess what they are? We'll come through in a minute.'

And, as they ran excitedly out of the room, he met Amelia's eyes and they both let out their breath on a soft laugh.

'Kids,' he said, and she nodded, her smile touched with sadness. On his behalf, he realised, and wanted to hug her. Nothing to do with those crazy cat pyjamas under a baggy old jumper that made him want to peel it off over her head and unwrap her as his very own Christmas present.

He cleared his throat. 'Right, how about that tea?'

'Sounds great. What on earth are you doing up this early, by the way?' she added as he went over to the kettle, and she sounded slightly amazed.

'Making tea, letting the dog out.'

'I'm sorry, I didn't hear him.'

'He didn't make a sound, but I was awake and I wanted to see the snow.'

'You surprise me. I wouldn't have thought you were best friends with snow at the moment.'

He chuckled. 'It wasn't the snow's fault. It was the idiot skiing up above me, but we were well off piste and if I hadn't had an avalanche kit with airbags to help me float on the snow cloud, it would have been very different. So, not the snow at fault, just someone who didn't know what they were doing, and anyway, it isn't often we have a white Christmas. Besides, I was already awake.'

She made a soft sound of sympathy. 'Couldn't you sleep?'

'On the contrary,' he told her, pouring their tea. 'I didn't think I'd sleep, but actually I slept better than I have for ages.'

'It must have been the whisky.'

'Maybe,' he agreed, but he knew it wasn't.

It had been the warmth—the human warmth from having a family in a house so obviously built with families in mind. And the fact that it had been a good day, and he'd enjoyed it. Well, most of it. The supermarket had been pretty hellish, but even that had had its high points. 'Here—' he said, handing her some tea, 'and there's a bottle for the baby cooling by the sink.'

'Oh, you star, thank you,' she said softly, sounding stunned. 'You didn't have to do that.'

'I knew he'd be awake soon. I made it according to the directions, so I hope it's all right and not too weak or strong. And it might still be a bit hot.'

'No, it's fine,' she said with a smile that threatened to send him into meltdown. Damn. Last night she was ripping him to shreds, and today he just wanted to undress her and carry her off to bed.

He took a step away and pretended to check the temperature on the Aga. 'What time do you want to put the turkey in?'

'It needs four hours in a moderate oven.'

He frowned at her. 'What does that mean?' he asked, and she laughed, the soft sound running through him like teasing fingertips.

'It means not too hot and not too cold. I'm sure it'll be fine. We've got ages. Why don't we go and see what the children are doing before they "accidentally" tear the paper?'

He chuckled and followed her, the dog trotting between them, not sure if he should be with the woman who fed him and loved him, or this new friend who'd taken him out in the magical white stuff and played with him. It occurred to Jake that he was having a good time—that, although he'd thought this would be his worst nightmare, in fact he was enjoying himself.

And that, in itself, was an amazing Christmas present.

He'd been wrong.

His presents weren't nothing. They were thoughtfully chosen, simple but absolutely perfect. Laura's had been extravagant, as she'd guessed, and just made her feel guilty and inadequate, and Kate's were very simple and sweet, the children's handmade by Megan, and an outrageous pair of frivolous lacy knickers for her to cheer her up, apparently—only she'd opened them in front of Jake and turned bright red with embarrassment and stuffed them in her pocket.

Her presents to the children had been things they needed, because there simply wasn't the money for anything else, but his—they were just fun, and the children were delighted.

'Oh, Mummy, look! It's that book I wanted!' Kitty said, eyes sparkling, and Millie looked up and met Jake's wary eyes and smiled apologetically.

'So it is. You'll have to be careful with the glitter, it goes everywhere. Say—'

But she didn't need to finish, because Kitty had thrown herself at Jake and hugged him hard. Very hard—hard enough to make him wince, but he was smiling, so she didn't think he minded.

'Edward, what's that?' she asked, watching her meticulous son peel away the last bit of wrapping and reveal his present.

'It's a kit to build all sorts of things—it's brilliant. Thank you, Jake!' her son said, and although he didn't hug him, his eyes were shining and she could see Jake was pleased that he'd got it right.

So very, very right. 'Thomas, look at this!' she exclaimed, unwrapping the shape sorter and giving it to him, and he picked it up and shook it and laughed happily.

'Tull!' he said, and Jake's face creased in bewilderment. 'Tull?'

'He thinks it's a rattle,' Edward explained. 'Look, Thomas, it opens, and you can put these bits in. See this one? It's a square. Look!'

And Thomas stared, fascinated, as the little shape went into the hole as if by magic, and Jake stared, just as fascinated, it seemed, and Millie blinked away the tears and looked back under the tree. There were still two presents there, and Kitty dived under and pulled them out.

'This is for Rufus, and this one's for you,' she said, handing Millie a soft, squashy parcel.

'Me?' she said, horribly conscious that she hadn't bought him anything, or made him anything or in fact done anything except make his already difficult life even harder.

She swallowed and met his eyes, and he smiled tentatively. 'Go on, open it. It's only silly.'

'I haven't—'

'Shh. Open it.'

So she did, and when she saw the fingerless mitts that could turn into proper mittens, her eyes filled. He'd listened to what she'd said about not being able to do anything with gloves on, and he'd found her a solution.

A silly, crazy pink solution, with a matching scarf that was soft and cosy and gorgeous, and her eyes flooded with tears that she could no longer hold back.

'You've made Mummy cry,' Kitty said, staring at her, and Edward looked at her worriedly, but she dredged up a smile and scrubbed her cheeks with the heels of her hands and met Jake's eyes.

'I'm fine, really. Thank you, Jake. Thank you for everything.'

'My pleasure,' he said. 'What about the dog's?'

'I hope it's not food.'

'It's not food. Here, open it,' he said, handing it to her, and she knelt up beside him and tore off the paper and her eyes filled again.

'It's a coat!' she said, choked. 'Oh, thank you, he's been miserable in the cold and he hates the rain. Oh, that's lovely.'

And then, because she couldn't hold back any longer, she leant over and hugged him. Not as hard as Kitty, careful of his bruises, but hard enough that he would know she really meant it.

And he hugged her back, his arms warm and hard and strong around her, and it would have been so easy to sink into them and stay there for the rest of the day.

The rest of her life.

No!

She straightened up, blinking away fresh tears and scrambling to her feet. 'Right, let's put all this paper in the bin and tidy up, and then we need to get dressed, and come back down and have breakfast, and then we've got the world's biggest snowman to build!'

CHAPTER SEVEN

It was the most magical day.

They'd all gone upstairs to wash and dress, and Jake had called her back and asked her to help him.

'I could do with a shower, but I don't want to get the new cast wet and I didn't do so well yesterday. Could you tape this bag over my arm?'

'Of course,' she said, putting Thomas on the floor, and he handed her the bag and some tape, and then shucked off his robe so he was standing in front of her in nothing more than snug-fitting jersey boxers that sent her heart rate rocketing. Until she saw his bruises, and they took her breath away.

'Oh, Jake—you're black and blue!'

He smiled wryly. 'Tell me about it. Still, I'm alive. It could have been worse. And it's better today.'

She wasn't convinced, but she stuck the bag on his arm and stood back, trying not to look at him and not really succeeding, because her eyes were relentlessly drawn to his taut, well-muscled chest with its scatter of dark curls, to the strong, straight legs with their spectacular muscles and equally spectacular bruises. 'Can you manage now?' she asked, trying to sound businesslike and obviously failing, because his right eyebrow twitched.

'Why?' he asked, his voice low and his eyes dancing with mischief. 'Are you offering to wash my back?'

'On second thoughts,' she said and, scooping Thomas up, she left him to it and concentrated—barely—on dressing her children and making breakfast for them all before she put Thomas down for a nap and they wrapped up warmly and went out into the snow.

The snowman was huge—probably not the biggest in the world, but huge for all that—and Jake had found his old ski hat and scarf and they'd raided the fridge for a carrot—and two sprouts for his eyes, 'because,' Kitty said, 'they're too disgusting to eat.' Edward found a twig that looked like a pipe to stick in his mouth. Then, when the snowman was finished, standing in pride of place outside the breakfast room window so he could watch them eat, they came back inside, hung their coats in the boiler room to dry, and settled down by the fire in the drawing room to watch a film while they warmed up.

She flitted between the film and the kitchen, making sure everything was set in motion at the right time like a military operation and laying the table in the breakfast room, because, as Jake said, the dining room was too formal for having fun in. Not to mention too beautiful for Thomas to hurl his dinner across the room or for Kitty to 'accidentally' shoot peas off the edge of her plate for the dog to find, and anyway, it was a long way from the kitchen.

So she put out the crackers and the cutlery and the jolly red and green paper napkins with reindeer on, and a big white pillar candle they'd bought in the supermarket standing on a red plate. In between doing that and checking on the meal, she sat with her family and Jake, squeezing up next to Edward, while Thomas sat wedged between him and Jake, and Kitty had found herself a little place on Jake's lap, with his arm round her and her head on his shoulder and her thumb in her mouth. The next time she came in he had Thomas on his lap instead, standing on his leg and trying to climb over the arm of the sofa.

'I think he's bored,' Jake said softly, and Thomas looked up at her and beamed and held up his arms, and she scooped him up and hugged him.

'Hungry too, probably.'

'Is it lunchtime yet?' Kitty asked hopefully. 'I'm *starving*!'

'Nearly.'

'Can I help?'

Could he? Could she cope with him in the kitchen, that strong, hard, battered body so close to hers in the confined space?

She nearly laughed. What was she thinking about? It wasn't confined, it was huge—but it had seemed confined this morning, while he was making her tea and she was in the pyjamas he'd teased her about and he was in a robe with melted snow on the shoulders and dripping off his hair and those curiously sexy bare feet planted squarely on the tiled floor.

And now she knew what had been under that robe, it would be all the harder...

'I don't really know what you can do,' she said, but he followed her anyway, and he managed one-handed to make himself very useful. He helped lift the turkey out of the dish, entertained Thomas while she warmed his lunch, and then blew on it and fed him while she made the gravy and put everything out into the serving dishes he'd found for her.

'Lunch!' she called, sticking her head round the door, and they came pelting down the hall and skidded into the breakfast room.

'Oh, it looks really pretty!' Kitty said. Jake lit the candle and she carried in the turkey and knew how Tiny Tim's mother must have felt when Scrooge gave them the goose.

The food was delicious, and the children piled in, eating themselves to a standstill, and still there was enough there to feed an army.

'I hope you've got a nice line in leftover recipes,' Jake murmured as he carried it out to the kitchen and put it on the side, making her laugh.

'Oh, I have. I can turn anything into a meal. Have you got any brandy to put over the pudding?'

'I have—and holly. I picked it this morning. Here.'

He turned off the lights, and she carried in the flaming pudding by candlelight, making the children ooh and aah. Then, when they couldn't manage another mouthful, they cleared the table and put on their warm, dry coats and went back out in the garden for a walk, with Rufus in his smart new tartan coat and Thomas snuggled on her hip in his all-in-one suit. When the children had run around and worked off their lunch and the adults had strolled all down the long walk from the house towards the woods, they turned back.

And, right in the middle of the lawn outside the bay window, Kitty stopped.

'We have to make snow angels!' she said. 'Come on, everybody!'

'Snow angels?' Jake said, his voice taut, and Millie looked at him worriedly. Was this another memory they were trampling on? Oh, dear lord—

'Yes—all of us! Come on, Jake, you're the biggest, you can be the daddy angel!'

And, oblivious to the shocked reluctance on his face, she dragged him by the arm, made him lie down, and lay down beside him with her arms and legs outstretched and fanned them back and forth until she'd cleared the snow, and then she got up, laughing and pulled him to his feet.

'Look! You're so big!' she said with a giggle. 'Mummy, you lie down there on the other side, and then Edward, and Thomas, too—'

'Not Thomas, darling, he's too small, he doesn't understand.'

'Well, Jake can hold him while you and Edward make your snow angels,' she said, bossy and persistent to the last. She looked into Jake's eyes and saw gentle resignation.

'I'll take him,' he said softly and, reaching out, he scooped him onto his right hip and held him firmly, one-handed, while she and Edward carved out their shapes in the snow, and then she took her baby back and they went inside to look, shedding their wet clothes all over again, only this time their trousers were wet as well, and they had to go up and change.

'Hey, you guys, come and look,' Jake called from his room, and they followed him in and stood in the bay window looking down on the little row of snow angels.

'That's so pretty!' Kitty said. 'Jake, take a picture!'

So he got out his phone and snapped a picture, then went along the landing and took another of the snowman. Afterwards they all went downstairs again and Kitty got out her book, and Edward got out the construction kit, and they set them up at the far end of the breakfast table and busied themselves while she loaded the dishwasher and cleared up the pots and pans.

There was no sign of Jake, but at least Thomas in his cot had stopped grizzling and settled into sleep.

Or so she thought, until Jake appeared in the doorway with her little son on his hip.

'He's a bit sorry for himself,' Jake said with a tender smile, and handed him over. 'Why don't you sit down and I'll make you a cup of tea?'

'Because I'm supposed to be looking after you and all you've done is make me tea!'

'You've been on your feet all day. Go on, shoo. I'll do it. Anyway, I can't sit, I'm too full.'

She laughed at that, and took Thomas through to the breakfast room, put him in his high chair with his shape sorter puzzle and sat down with the children while she waited for her tea.

'Mummy, I can't do this. I can't work it out,' Edward said, staring at the instructions and the zillions of pieces he was trying to put together. It was complicated—more complicated than anything he'd tackled yet, but she was sure he'd be able to do it.

And how clever of Jake to realise that he was very bright, she thought, as she saw the kit was for older children. Bright and brave and hugely talented in all sorts of ways, and yet his father couldn't see it—just saw a quiet child with nothing to say for himself and no apparent personality.

Well, it was his loss, she thought, but of course it wasn't—it was Edward's, too, that he was so undervalued by the man who should have been so proud of him, should have nurtured and encouraged him. It wouldn't have occurred to David to look into choir school. He would have thought it was sissy.

But there was nothing—*nothing*—sissy about Jake. In fact he was a lot like Edward—thorough, meticulous, paying attention to detail, noticing the little things, fixing stuff, making it right.

The nurturer, she realised, and wondered if he'd spent his childhood trying to stick his family back together again when clearly, from what she'd overheard, it had been broken beyond repair. How sad that when he'd found his own, it had been torn away from him.

And then he came out and sat down with them all, on the opposite side of the table, and slid the tea across to her. Edward looked up at him and said, 'Can you give me a hand?'

'Sure. What's the problem?' he asked, and bent his head over the instructions, sorted through the pieces and found the missing bit. 'I think this needs to go in here,' he said, and handed it to Edward. Didn't take over, didn't do it for him, did just enough to help him on his way and then sat back and let him do it.

He did, of course, bit by bit, with the occasional input from Jake to keep him on the straight and narrow, but there was a worrying touch of hero worship in his voice. She only hoped they could all get through this and emerge unscathed without too many broken hopes and dreams, because, although Jake was doing nothing she could fault, Edward was lapping up every moment of his attention, desperate for a father figure in his life, for a man who understood him.

And she was dreading the day they moved out, to wherever they ended up, and she had to take him away from Jake.

She doubted Jake was dreading it. He was putting up with the invasion of his privacy with incredible fortitude, but she had no doubts at all that he'd be glad when they left and he could settle back into his own routine without all the painful reminders.

Sadly, she didn't think it would be any time soon, but all too quickly reality was going to intervene and she'd have to start sending out her CV again and trying to get another job. Maybe Jake would let her use the Internet so she could do that.

But not now. It was Christmas, and she was going to keep smiling and make sure everyone enjoyed it.

Jake included.

He thought the day would never end.

It had been fun—much more fun than he could have imagined—but it was also painful. Physically, because he was still sore from his encounter with the trees and the rocks in France, and emotionally, because the kids were great and it just underlined exactly what he'd lost.

And until that day, he'd avoided thinking about it, had shut his heart and his mind to such thoughts.

But he couldn't shut them out any more; they seeped in, like light round the edges of a blind, and while Millie was putting the children to bed he went into his little sitting room and closed the door. There was a video of them all taken on Ben's second birthday, and he'd never watched it again, but it was there, tormenting him.

So he put it on, and he watched his little son and the wife he'd loved to bits laughing into the camera, and he let the tears fall. Healing tears—tears that washed away the pain and left bittersweet memories of happier days. Full days.

Days like today.

And then he took the DVD out and put it away again, and lay down on the sofa and dozed. He was tired, he realised. He'd slept well last night, but not for long, and today had been a long day. He'd go to bed later, but for now he was comfortable, and if he kept out of the way Amelia wouldn't feel she had to talk to him when she'd rather be doing something—probably anything—else.

She'd done well. Brilliantly. The meal had been fabulous, and he was still full. Maybe he'd have a sandwich later, start on the pile of cold turkey that would be on the menu into the hereafter. Turkey and cold stuffing and cranberry sauce.

But later. Not now. Now, he was sleeping…

'That was the *best* day,' Edward said, snuggling down under the quilt and smiling at her. 'Jake's really cool.'

'He's been very kind,' she said, wondering how she could take Jake gently off this pedestal without shattering Edward's illusions, 'but we are in his way.'

'He doesn't seem to mind.'

'That's because he's a very kind man, very generous.'

'That's what Kate said—that he was generous.' He

rolled onto his back and folded his arms under his head. 'Did you know he went to choir school?'

'Yes—I heard him tell you,' she said. 'I'd just come downstairs.'

'He said it was great. Hard work, but he loved it there. He was a boarder, did you know that? He had to sleep there, but he said his mum and dad used to fight, and he was always in the way, so it was good, really.'

She was just opening her mouth to comment when Edward went on diffidently, 'Were we in the way? Was that why Dad left?'

Her heart aching, she hugged him. 'No, darling. He left because he realised he didn't love me any more, and it wouldn't have been right to stay.'

He hadn't loved the children either, but there was no way she was telling Edward that his father had used them as a lever to get her to agree to things she wouldn't otherwise have countenanced. Things like remortgaging their house so riskily, because otherwise, he said, they'd be homeless.

Well, they were homeless now, and he'd had to flee the country to escape the debt, so a lot of good it had done to prolong it. And why on earth she'd let him back last year so that she'd ended up pregnant again, she couldn't imagine. She must have been insane, and he'd gone again long before she'd realised about the baby.

Not that she'd send Thomas back, not for a moment, but life had become infinitely more complicated with another youngster.

She'd have to work on her CV, she thought, and wondered what Jake was doing and if he'd let her use the

Internet to download a template so she could lay it out better.

'You need to go to sleep,' she said softly, and bent over and kissed Edward's cheek. 'Come on, snuggle down.'

'Can we play in the snow again tomorrow?' he asked sleepily, and she nodded.

'Of course—if it's still there.'

'It will be. Jake said.'

And if Jake had said...

She went out and pulled the door to, leaving the landing light on for them, and after checking on the sleeping baby she went back downstairs, expecting to find Jake in the breakfast room or the drawing room.

But he wasn't, and his study door was open, and his bedroom door had been wide open, too.

Which left his little sitting room. His cave, the place to which he retreated from the world when it all became too much.

She didn't like to disturb him, so she put her laptop in the breakfast room and tidied up the kitchen. The children had had a snack, and she was pretty sure that Jake would want something later, so she made a pile of sandwiches with freshly cut bread, and wrapped them in cling film and put them in the fridge ready for him. Then she put Rufus's new coat on and took him out into the snow for a run around.

He should have been used to it, he'd been outside several times today, but still he raced around and barked and tried to bite it, and she stood there feeling the cold seep into her boots and laughed at him as he played.

And then she turned and saw Jake standing in the

window of his sitting room, watching her with a brooding expression on his face, and she felt her heart miss a beat.

Their eyes locked, and she couldn't breathe, frozen there in time, waiting for—

What? For him to summon her? To call her to him, to ask her to join him?

Then he glanced away, his gaze caught by the dog, and she could breathe again.

'Rufus!' she called, and she took him back inside, dried his paws on an old towel and took off her snowy boots and left them by the Aga to dry off. And as she straightened up, he came into the kitchen.

'Hi. All settled?'

She nodded. 'Yes. Yes, they're all settled. I wasn't sure if you'd be hungry, so I made some sandwiches.'

'Brilliant. Thanks. I was just coming to do that, but I wasn't sure if I could cut the bread with one hand. It's all a bit awkward.'

'Done,' she said, opening the fridge and lifting them out. 'Do you want them now, or later?'

'Now?' he said. 'Are you going to join me? I thought maybe we could have a glass of wine and a little adult conversation.'

His smile was wry, and she laughed softly, her whole body responding to the warmth in his eyes.

'That would be lovely,' she said, and found some plates while he opened the bottle of red they'd started the night before last and poured two glasses, and they carried them through to the breakfast room, but then he hesitated.

'Come and slum it with me on the sofa,' he suggested,

to her surprise, and she followed him through to the other room and sat down at one end while he sprawled into the other corner, his sore leg—well, the sorer of the two, if the bruises were anything to go by—stretched out so that his foot was almost touching her thigh.

And they ate their sandwiches and talked about the day, and then he put his plate down on the table beside him and said, 'Tell me about your work.'

'I don't have any,' she reminded him. 'In fact, I was going to ask you about that. I need to write a CV and get it out to some firms. I don't suppose you've got wireless broadband so I can go online and do some research?'

'Sure. You can do it now, if you like. I'll help you—if you want.'

She flashed him a smile. 'That would be great. Thanks.'

'Any time. Have you got a computer or do you want to use mine?'

'My laptop—it's in the breakfast room. I'll get it.'

He'd sat up by the time she got back in there, so she ended up sitting close to him, his solid, muscled thigh against hers, his arm slung along the back of the sofa behind her. As she brought up her CV, he glanced at it and sat back.

'OK, I can see a few problems with it. It needs more immediacy, it needs to grab the attention. You could do with a photo of yourself, for a start. People like to know who they're dealing with.'

'Really? For freelance? It's not as if I'd have to disgrace their office—'

'Disgrace? Don't be ridiculous,' he said, leaving her feeling curiously warm inside. 'And anyway, it's about how you look at the camera, if you're open and straight-forward and decent.'

'Or if you have tattoos or a ton of shrapnel in your face,' she added, but he laughed and shook his head.

'That's irrelevant unless you're talking front of house and it's the sort of organisation where it matters. In some places it'd be an asset. It's much more about connecting with the photo. Stay there.'

And he limped out stiffly, drawing her attention to the fact that he was still sore, despite all he'd done today for her and her children. He should have been lying down taking it easy, she thought uncomfortably, not making snowmen and snow angels and construction toys. And now her CV.

He came back with another laptop, flipped it open and logged on, and then scrolled through his files and brought up his own CV. 'Here—this is me. I can't show you anyone else's, it wouldn't be fair, but this is the basic stuff—fonts, the photo size and so on.'

She scanned it, much more interested in the personal information than anything else. His date of birth—he was a Cancerian, she noticed, and thirty-five this year, five years older than her—and he'd been born in Norwich, he had three degrees, he was crazily clever and his interests were diverse and, well, interesting.

She scanned through it and sat back.

'Wow. You're pretty well qualified.'

'So are you. How come you can't find a job? Is it that they don't get beyond the CV?'

She laughed. 'What, a single woman with three young children and one of them under a year?'

'But people aren't allowed to ask that sort of thing.'

'No, but they ask about how much time you're able to commit and can you give weekends and evenings if necessary, are you available for business trips—all sorts of sly manoeuvring to get it out of you, and then you can hear the gates slam shut.'

'That's crazy. Lots of my key people are mothers, and they tend to be well-organised, efficient and considerate. And OK, from time to time I have to make concessions, but they don't pull sickies because they've drunk too much the night before, and they don't get bored and go off travelling. There are some significant advantages. I'd take you on.'

She stared at him, not sure if he'd meant that quite how it sounded, because Kate had said in the past that it was a shame he had someone and didn't need her. So it was probably just a casual remark. But it might not have been...

'You would?' she asked tentatively, and he nodded.

'Sure. I could do with a translator. It's not technical stuff, it's more business contract work, but I farm it out at the moment to someone I've used for years and she told me before Christmas that she wants a career break. What languages have you got?'

'French, Italian, Spanish and Russian.'

He nodded slowly. 'OK. Want to try? Have a look at some of the things I need translating and see if you've got enough of the specific vocabulary to do it?'

'Sure,' she said slowly, although she wasn't sure. She wasn't sure at all if it would be a good thing to do, to become even more involved with a man who her son thought had hung the moon and the stars, and on whose lap her daughter had spent a good part of the day cuddled up in front of the fire.

A man whose heart was so badly broken that he had to run away every Christmas and hide from the pain.

A man, she realised, who she could very easily come to love...

He must be crazy.

It was bad enough having them all descend on him without a by-your-leave, taking over his house and his life and his mind. It was only a step from lunacy to suggest a lasting liaison.

Not that it need be anything other than strictly professional, he realised. It could all be done online—in fact, it could be Kate who dealt with all the communications. He didn't have to do anything other than rubber-stamp payment of her invoices. It would solve her financial problems, give her independence from the scumbag of an ex-husband who'd trashed her life so comprehensively with his lousy judgement and wild ideas, and give the children security.

And that, he discovered, mattered more to him than he really wanted to admit. It would give them a chance to find a house, to settle into schools—and that in itself would give Edward a chance to join a choir, church or school, or maybe even apply to choir schools for a scholarship. They could live anywhere they chose, because she wouldn't have to come into the office, and so if he did end up in a choir school he wouldn't necessarily have to board if she was close enough to run around after him.

And she could afford to look after Rufus.

He glanced down at the dog, snuggled up between their feet, utterly devoted to his mistress.

Hell, he'd miss the dog when they moved. Miss all of them. He'd have to think about getting a dog. He'd considered it in the past but dismissed it because of his business visitors who stayed in the house from time to time, but maybe it was time to think about himself, to put himself first, to admit, perhaps, that he, too, had needs.

And feelings.

'Think about it, and we'll go over some stuff tomorrow, maybe,' he said, shutting his laptop and getting to his feet. 'I'm going to turn in.'

'Yes, it's been a long day.' She shut her own laptop and stood up beside him, gathering up their glasses with her free hand. Then, while she put the dog out, he put his computer back in the study and went back to the kitchen, looking broodingly out over the garden at the snowman staring back at him with slightly crooked Brussels sprout eyes, and he wondered if his feelings could extend to a relationship.

Not sex, not just another casual, meaningless affair, a way to scratch an itch, to blank out the emptiness of his life, but a relationship.

With Amelia.

She was calling Rufus, patting her leg and encouraging him away from a particularly fascinating smell, and then the door shut and he heard the key turn and she came through to the breakfast room and stopped.

'Oh! I thought you'd gone upstairs.'

'No. I was waiting for you,' he said, and something

flickered in her eyes, an acknowledgement of what he might have said.

He led her to the landing by his bedroom and turned to her, staring wordlessly down at her for the longest moment. It was crazy. He didn't know her, he wasn't ready, he was only now starting to sift through the raft of feelings left behind by losing his family—but he wanted her, her and her family, and he didn't know how to deal with that.

Sex he could handle. This—this was something else entirely. He lifted his right hand and cradled her cheek. 'Thank you for today,' he said softly, and her eyes widened and she shook her head.

'No—thank *you*, Jake. You've been amazing—so kind I don't know how to start. It could have all been unimaginably awful, and instead—it's been the best Christmas I can remember. And it's all down to you. So thank you, for everything you've done, for me, for the children, even for Rufus. You're a star, Jake Forrester—a good man.'

And, going up on tiptoe, she pressed a soft, tentative kiss to his lips.

The kiss lingered for a second, and then her heels sank back to the floor, taking her away from him, and he took a step back and let her go with reluctance.

There was time, he told himself as he got ready for bed. There was no hurry—and maybe this was better not hurried, but given time to grow and develop over time.

He opened the bedside drawer and took out his painkillers, and the photo caught his eye. He lifted it out and stared at them. They seemed like strangers now, distant memories, part of his past. He'd never forget them, but they were gone, and maybe he was ready to move on.

He opened his suitcase and pulled out the broken remains of the watch, and put it with the photograph in a box full of Rachel's things in the top of his wardrobe.

Time to move on, he told himself.

With Amelia?

CHAPTER EIGHT

'Isn't it time we bathed the dog? We've been talking about it for days, and we still haven't got round to it.'

She looked up at Jake and bit her lip to stop the smile. 'He is pretty smelly, isn't he?'

'You could say that. And right now he's wet and mucky from the snow, so it seems like a good time. And he's got all night to dry by the fire.'

'I'll get my shampoo and conditioner and run the water in the sink,' she said, getting to her feet from the hearthrug and running up to her bathroom, then coming back to the utility room—because even she drew the line at bathing the dog in the kitchen sink—and a moment later Jake appeared with the dog at his heels and an armful of towels from the cupboard in the boiler room.

'Here—old towels. I tend to use them for swimming, but I'm sure the dog won't object.'

They were better than her best ones, she thought, but she didn't comment, just thanked him, picked Rufus up and stood him in the water and ladled it over him with a plastic jug she'd found in the cupboard under the sink.

'He's very good,' Jake said, leaning against the worktop

and watching her bath him. 'Not that that surprises me. Did you have time to look at any of that stuff I gave you, by the way?'

'Yes. It doesn't look too bad. Do you want me to have a go?'

'Could you?'

'Sure. I'll do it while Rufus dries, if you like.' She lathered him from end to end, drenched him in conditioner to get the tangles out, then rinsed him again even more thoroughly and lifted the plug out and squeezed the water off him and then bundled him up in the towels and carried him back to the fire.

'Have you got a comb?'

'I'll brush him,' she said, and gently teased the tangles out while he stood and shivered.

'Is he cold?'

'No, he just hates it. He's a wuss and he doesn't like being brushed. He'll get over it.'

'Is she being mean to you, sweetheart?' he crooned, and Rufus wafted his skinny little tail, looking pleadingly at his hero for rescue.

'Forget it, big-eyes, you're getting brushed,' she said firmly, but she kissed him to take the sting out of it. It was over in a moment, and then he shook wildly and ran round the room, scrubbing his face on the rug and making them laugh.

'Right, those documents,' she said. 'Shall I do it on my computer?'

'It's probably easier.'

So she sat at the table, and he sat in the chair by the fire, and Rufus settled down on a towel and let Jake brush him gently until he was dry, and she thought how nice it was, how cosy—and she couldn't imagine what she was doing getting herself sucked into La-La Land like this.

So she forced herself to concentrate, and after a while she sat back and blew out her cheeks.

'OK, I've done it.'

'What, the first one?'

'No, all three.'

'Really?'

He sat next to her, produced the translations he'd already apparently had done and scanned the two side by side, and then sat back and met her eyes.

'They're excellent. Better. Better English—cleaner, clearer. So—do you want the job?'

She laughed a little breathlessly. 'Do I—I don't know. That depends on what you pay, and how.' And how much contact I'll have to have with you, and whether it's going to do my head in trying to be sensible—

'Word count, normally. I'm not sure what we pay without looking, but I'm sure it's fair, and if you don't agree with it, I'll match what you've been getting. That's on top of a retainer, of course. I can check for you. I'll have a look through the accounts. We can go over to the office tomorrow—in fact, do you think the kids would like to swim? The pool's there doing nothing, and you'll have it to yourselves unless any of the staff come over to use it, but I would have thought they're unlikely to do so this soon after Christmas. It's up to you.'

'Oh. They'd love to swim,' she said ruefully, contemplating the idea of being on a retainer because her last job had been much more hit and miss than that, 'but they haven't got any costumes. Swimwear wasn't top of my list of priorities when I was packing things up to go into storage. I have no idea where they'd be, either.'

'It doesn't matter. They can swim in pants. So can you. Bra and pants is only what a bikini is, and I promise I won't look.'

She felt her cheeks heat and looked away from his teasing eyes. Since she'd kissed him last night, she'd scarcely been able to think about anything else, and for the whole day it had been simmering between them. It wasn't just her, she was sure of it, but he didn't seem to be about to take it any further, and goodness knows she shouldn't be encouraging him to.

The last thing—well, almost the last thing, anyway— she needed was to get involved in a complicated relationship with the first person to offer her work in months. And she needed a job more than she needed sex.

Except it wasn't that, or it didn't feel like it. It felt like— help, it felt dangerously like love, and that was so scary she couldn't allow herself to think about it. She'd had it with rich, flashy, ruthless men.

Not that he was flashy, not in the least, but he was certainly rich, and however generous he might have been to her, she was sure that Jake could be ruthless when it suited him or the occasion demanded it. Heavens, she knew he could, she'd been on the receiving end of his ruthless tongue on the first night!

But that had been him lashing out, sore and tired and a little desperate, at someone who'd come uninvited into his home, his retreat, his sanctuary. No wonder.

Nevertheless, it was there, that ruthless streak, and

David's ruthlessness had scarred her and her children in a way that she was sure would never completely fade.

'It's not such a hard question, is it?' he murmured, jerking her back to the present, and she met his eyes in confusion.

'What isn't?'

'Swimming,' he reminded her gently. 'What did you think I was talking about?'

She had no idea. She'd been so far away, reliving the horror of David's heartless and uncaring defection, that she'd forgotten all about the swim he'd talked of.

She tried to smile. 'I'm sorry, I was wool-gathering. No, it's not hard. I'm sure the children would both love to swim, but you can't, can you, with the cast on?' And there was no way she was swimming in pants—most especially not the pants Kate had given her!

'No. No, of course not, but it's sitting there. I just thought they might enjoy it. And I'd like to show you the office. Not that you'll be working there necessarily, but you might find it interesting to see the place.'

She would. She found everything about him interesting, and that was deeply worrying. But she accepted, telling herself that it would give her a better insight into his business operation and help her make a more informed decision about whether to take the job or not.

In fact, maybe she should talk to Kate, and she vowed to do that as soon as she had a chance. But, in the meantime, she'd have a look at his offices, let the kids have a swim and think about it.

The following morning, after the children were washed and dressed and she'd taped up Jake's cast so he could shower, and once they'd had breakfast and walked the squeaky-clean Rufus in his smart little coat, they went over to the old country club site and he let them into the offices hidden away behind the walls of the old kitchen garden.

'Sorry, it's a bit chilly. The heating's turned down but we won't be in here long and the pool area's warm,' he said, and pushed open a door into what had to be his office. There was a huge desk, a vast window and the same beautiful view down the long walk that the drawing room and his bedroom enjoyed. A long, low sofa stretched across one wall, and she guessed he sprawled on it often when he was working late, a coffee in his hand, checking emails on his laptop or talking on the phone.

She pictured him pacing, gesturing, holding everything in his head while he negotiated and wrangled until he was satisfied that he'd got the best deal. She'd seen David do it, seen the way he worked, the way he pinned people down and bullied them until he got his way, and a chill ran over her.

Was Jake like that? The iron hand in the velvet glove? She didn't like to think so, but even a pussycat had claws, and Jake was no pussycat. He could be tough and uncompromising, she was sure, and that made her deeply uneasy. But then wasn't everyone who'd survived in business in these difficult times? And she needed that job.

'Come on, kids, more to see and then there's the pool,' he was saying. They scrambled off his sofa and ran back to the door, and she followed them, Thomas in the stroller so she could have her hands free to help the children when they had their swim.

'This is the main office, this is Kate's office, this is reception—I brought you in the back way, but visitors come in via this door from the garden,' he explained, opening it so that the children could go out and run around in the snow, and she looked out over a pretty scene of snow-covered lawn surrounded by what looked like roses climbing up against the mellow brick walls. In the centre was a little fountain. The children were chasing each other round it, giggling and shrieking and throwing snowballs, and she smiled, relieved to see them so happy after such a difficult year.

'It's beautiful. It must be lovely in the summer.'

'It is. The staff sit out there for their coffee and lunch breaks. It's a lovely place to work, and I knew it would be. I saw it just before—' He broke off, then went on, 'I saw it five and a half years ago, and I was committed to it, so I just shifted my plans a little and went ahead anyway, and it's been a good move—and the right one, although I had no choice because the house was sold and we'd started work on this already.'

'That must have been hard,' she said softly, and he shrugged.

'Not really. We'd made the decision. It was the house that was so hard to deal with. We got the builders in and started at the top. We'd planned to live in the rooms up there at first, so that was already commissioned, and then—well, I got an interior designer in to do the rest, but I wouldn't let her interfere with that bit. It went ahead as planned, and I made it the place where people with children stay, because that was always the idea. We were going to put a kitchen up there as a temporary measure but of course that never happened and I lived somewhere else while it was all done and concentrated on the offices at first.'

He was standing staring at the house, visible over the top of the garden wall, his hands in his pockets, a brooding expression on his face, and she turned away, giving him privacy. Why on earth was she imagining he'd be interested in a relationship with her? Of course he wasn't. He was still in love with his wife—the wife with whom he'd planned the rooms she and her family were living in now.

Of all the rooms for them to have chosen—but maybe it was a good thing. It showed that the plans had been right, and Kate, who didn't know about his wife and son, loved the rooms, too, and had stayed there. And he'd designated it the area for families, so maybe she was just being oversensitive.

What was she thinking? Did she like the set-up, or was she just being polite? Or did she genuinely like it but didn't want to work with him?

Too complicated, too much baggage for both of them?

'We need to talk terms,' he said, hoping that he could coax her into it and that, once coaxed, she would have time to get used to him, to find out the kind of man he was, to learn to trust him. Because she must have trust issues after a bastard like David Jones had messed so comprehensively with her life.

But he couldn't rush her, he knew that. All he could do was make it possible for her to live again, to give her time to draw breath, to get back on her feet. And maybe then—

His phone rang and he pulled it impatiently out of his

pocket and glanced at the screen. Kate. He felt a flicker of guilt but dismissed it and answered the call.

'Well, hello there. Had a good Christmas?'

'Yes…Jake, can we talk?'

'Why? What's wrong?' he asked, suddenly concerned that something might have happened to her.

She just gave a strangled laugh. 'What's wrong?' she exclaimed. 'You told me I hadn't heard the end of it, and I haven't heard a thing from you since, and the last time I spoke to you, you were injured and hopping mad. I didn't know if you were all right, if you'd forgiven me, if I'd even got a job to come back to. So of course I didn't have a good Christmas, you idiot! Oh, I'm sorry, I didn't mean to say that, but—really, Jake, I've been so worried and you didn't return my call, and you always do.'

Damn. He should have rung her. He'd meant to, so many times, but his eye had been so firmly off the ball—

'I'm sorry. I meant to ring. Of course you've got a job. Look, why don't you bring Megan over for a swim and have a chat and a coffee? In fact, swing by a sports shop and pick up some swimming things for Amelia and the kids on the way here. Theirs are in store. See you in—what? An hour?'

'Less—much less. I've got a costume Millie can use, and one of Megan's that Kitty can borrow, so I only need to get something for Edward and I might be able to find something here of his he left behind in the summer. I'll see you soon,' she said, and hung up.

He put the phone back in his pocket and turned to Amelia. 'That was Kate,' he said unnecessarily. 'She's coming over now with swimming things for all of you.'

'I gathered. Did she really think she might not have a job?' Amelia asked, frowning worriedly. 'Sorry, I didn't mean to eavesdrop, but I couldn't help overhearing your remark. I've been meaning to ring. I had a missed call from her on my phone, and I meant to ring her back, but—'

'Ditto. We've been dealing with other things. Don't worry, she's fine. She's far too valuable for me to lose, and she knows that. Or I hope she knows that.'

'I don't know that she does. She certainly doesn't take you for granted. I think she feels you're a bit of a miracle.'

'Me?' He gave a startled laugh and thought about it. 'I'm no miracle. I'm a tough boss. Make no mistake about that, Amelia. I don't pull punches. I expect my staff to work hard, but no harder than I do, and if they give me their best, I'll defend them to the hilt. But I don't suffer fools.'

Fools like her husband. Correction—*ex*-husband. Thank God he was in Thailand, it'd save him the effort of driving him out of the country.

'Jake? Does she know? About your family?'

He shook his head. 'No. Hardly anybody does. A few who've known me for years, but they don't talk about it and neither do I, we all just get on with it.'

'OK. Just so I know not to say anything. I thought she probably didn't because we talked about you and she didn't mention it, but I don't want to put my foot in it and you've obviously got your reasons for not telling everyone.'

He shrugged. 'It's just never come up. Work is work. I don't talk about myself.'

'But you talk about them. Kate said you always ask about Megan, and about other people's families, and you give very generous maternity deals and so on, and you send flowers when people are sick, and when Kate's pipes froze you put them up in the house—so it's only yourself you keep at arm's length,' she pointed out—probably fairly, now he thought about it.

He gave her a smile that felt slightly off-kilter. 'It's just easier that way. I don't want sympathy, Amelia. I don't need it. I just want to be left alone to live my life.'

Except suddenly that wasn't true any more, he acknowledged, feeling himself frown. He didn't want to be left alone. He wanted—

'Can we see the pool now?'

Kitty was under his nose, covered in snow, her cheeks bright and glowing with health, her eyes sparkling, and behind her Edward was stamping snow off his boots and shutting the door and watching him hopefully.

'Sure. Kate rang. She's bringing Megan over and some swimming things for you all. She'll be here in a minute.'

'Yippee, yippee, we're going in the pool!' Kitty sang, and Edward was laughing.

'That's amazing. We've just had a snowball fight and now we're going swimming! That's so weird. Are you coming in?'

He shook his head. 'I can't—my cast,' he explained, lifting up his arm. 'I can't get it wet. But I can't wait. I swim every day at six before everyone gets here, and I really miss it. So you won't mind if I don't watch you, because I'll just get jealous. You guys go ahead and have a really good time, OK?'

And then Kate arrived with Megan, to the children's delight, and he took one look at her and went over and hugged her.

'Hey, smile for me,' he said, holding her by the shoulders and looking down into her eyes. To his surprise, they filled with tears.

'I felt so awful, but I didn't know what to do, and I didn't think you'd mind. You weren't even supposed to be here—'

'Hey, it's fine. And you're right, I wouldn't have minded and you did absolutely the right thing, so stop worrying. I'd probably be more cross if you hadn't done what you did, so forget it. Anyway,' he said, changing the subject, 'the kids are dying to get in the pool, and I'd like a minute to talk to Amelia, so if you wouldn't mind keeping an eye on them. Amelia, is that OK with you?'

'Sure.' Amelia nodded, and Kate shot her a curious look.

'Right—sort yourselves out, and come and find me, Amelia. I'll be in my office.'

And he left them to it, turned up the heating in his office and checked his emails. Grief. There were loads, and he scrolled through them, deleting the majority without a second glance, saving a few, answering a couple.

And then she was there, standing in the doorway looking a little uneasy, and he switched off his machine and stood up.

'Come on in, I was just doing my email. Coffee?'

'Oh—thanks. Will you have any milk or should I go and get some?'

'Creamer. Is that OK?'

'Fine.' She crossed over to the window and stood staring down the long walk. 'How do you get any work done?' she asked softly, and he chuckled.

'It helps. There's nothing going on—well, apart from the odd squirrel. So my mind's free to think. It's good. No distractions, no diversions—it works for me. And it's peaceful. I love it best when there's nobody here, first thing in the morning and last thing at night.'

'And the house?' she asked, turning to face him.

'What about the house?'

'I get the feeling you sleep there.'

'And eat. Sometimes. And entertain. And I do spend time there, in my study or the sitting room. I don't use the rest of it much, it's a bit formal really.'

And lonely, but he didn't add that, because he didn't want to think about it, about how it hadn't been lonely for the last few days, and how empty and desolate it would feel when they were gone.

'I don't suppose you've thought about the job any more overnight?' he asked, handing her a coffee, and she took it and nodded, following him to the sofa and sitting down.

'Yes, but I need to know if it will be enough, if you can offer me enough work to live on. I don't want to be rude, and I'm not trying to push the rate up or anything, but I do need to earn a living and because my time's limited I need to maximise. And I am good, I know that. So I need to do the best I can for my family. I've been thinking about what you said about Edward, too, wondering if I could get him a voice test or singing lessons, but I need financial security before I even consider that. It's a juggling act, work time and quality time, although without the work the quality's pretty compromised so what am I talking about? But I do have to think about this and I know you're shut over

Christmas and New Year, so I don't know when you're thinking of me starting—'

'Whenever,' he said, cutting her off before she talked herself out of it. 'I can find you a pile of stuff. Judith—my translator—has been doing less recently, and there's a bit of a backlog, so if you want to start on that, I'd be very grateful. Some of it's probably getting a bit urgent.'

'So—would I submit an invoice when you're happy?'

'Or I can give you a cheque now,' he said. 'Just an advance, to start you off.' Which would give her enough money to find a rented house and move out, he realised with regret, but he couldn't hold her hostage, even if he wanted to.

'Don't you want references?' she was asking incredulously, and he laughed.

'No. You're a friend of Kate's, I've met your children, I've met your husband—'

'David? When did you meet David?' she asked, her voice shocked.

He shrugged. 'Last year? I believe it was him. He came to me with an idea he wanted to float for a coffee shop chain.'

'Oh, that's him. It was a crazy idea. I had no idea he'd approached you about it. I expect the fact Kate works for you put the idea into his head. Funny she didn't mention he'd been to see you.'

'She didn't know. I met him at a conference.'

'Oh. So what did you say?'

'I turned him down. It was ill-considered, risky and I didn't want to put my money there.' And he'd disliked the man on sight, but he didn't say that, because it was irrelevant and, after all, presumably she'd loved him once, although what came next made him wonder.

'Wise move,' she said, and smiled ruefully. 'Who knows what I saw in him, but by the time I realised what he was like it was too late, we were married and our second child was on the way. And when I tackled him about some things I'd found out, he walked.'

'And Thomas?'

'I let him come back. Don't ask me why, I have no idea. Maybe I felt I owed it to the children to give it another chance. It didn't last, and then when he'd gone—my idea, not his, because I realised he was relying on my income to support him—I discovered I was pregnant again. And that time I did divorce him. But what's David got to do with my job?'

'Just that I know the mess your life's in isn't your fault. I can imagine you trying to hold it all together, and I can imagine him selling it all out from under you without you realising. So I know you aren't in this position because you're incompetent, and you're right, you are good at your job. Quick and accurate. I need that—particularly the accuracy. The exact meaning of a contract is massively important, and although a lot of the stuff is standard, there are some sneaky little clauses. I like those dealt with, and I need to know what they are. So—I'm more than happy to take you on. My HR people will sort out the fine print when they get back, but in the meantime I'll give you the same rate Judith was on plus a twenty per cent enhancement and increase the retainer by forty per cent—I can find out exactly what that translates to in a minute, and you can start as soon as you like.'

She nodded slowly. 'OK. I need to see how the figures stack up. I might need to take on other work from somewhere else—'

'Don't do that,' he said, cutting her off. 'There's plenty of communication with foreign companies on a daily basis that we might need help with, as well as the really important stuff. French and Italian aren't too much of a problem—I speak them well enough for most things and so do a couple of others—but we struggle with Russian and our Spanish is on the weak side, so if you find you aren't earning enough, just shout. I could probably use you getting on for full-time, even maybe phone calls, that sort of thing. We do so much work abroad now and it would be really handy.'

She nodded thoughtfully. 'OK. Let me see the figures, and we'll talk again,' she said with a smile, and he felt the tension go out of his shoulders.

Good. He wasn't going to lose her—not entirely. He'd make sure of that, make sure the money was so tempting she would be mad to turn it down. She might move out once she'd got some financial security, but he could still phone her, ask her to explain something, find excuses to keep in touch personally—and now he was being ridiculous.

'Go and swim with your children. I'll look up the figures, find some material for you to start on and we'll go from there.'

He just hoped he could convince her...

CHAPTER NINE

'So what was that all about?'

She swam over to Kate and propped her arms on the edge of the pool. 'He's offered me a job. Apparently his translator wants to take a career break.'

'Judith? I didn't know that. Wow. Well, you've obviously made a good impression. I'm so sorry you ended up in that difficult situation with him before Christmas, by the way. I've been feeling so guilty, but you've obviously survived it. How did it go?'

How did it go? Between the tears and the heart-searching—

'OK. It was OK. Fun. He was brilliant. We went to the supermarket and bought loads of food, and I cooked Christmas lunch, and he bought the children little presents—he even got the dog a coat.'

'Good grief,' Kate said faintly. 'Still, it shouldn't really surprise me—when he does something, he usually does it well. He's a stickler for detail.'

'Hmm, that's what worries me about taking this job on. What if I'm not good enough?'

'You will be,' Kate said instantly. 'Of course you will

be. He's only got to look at your references to know that. Is he taking them up?'

'He says not.'

Kate's eyes widened, and then she started to laugh. 'Oh, my. Still, it's not the first time, he's a very good judge of character, but…Millie, I have a feeling he really likes you. As in, *likes* you.'

She shook her head. 'No. No way, Kate, it's too complicated. He isn't in the market for that sort of thing and neither am I.'

'How do you know? That he isn't, I mean? Did he say something?'

Damn. 'Well, he wouldn't be, would he?' she said, going for the obvious in the interests of preserving his privacy. 'Three kids and a dog? You'd be insane to want to take that on. And besides, what would I want with another entrepreneur? I've had it with living my life on a knife-edge, waiting for the next roll of the stock market dice to see if I'll be homeless or not. I want security, Kate, and I don't need a man for that. But I will take his job, and as soon as I can I'll find a house and get out of his hair and get our life back on track. Get the kids enrolled in a new school, and start again. And hopefully, this time it'll last longer than a few months.'

'So what's for supper?' he asked, coming up behind her and peering over her shoulder as she stirred the pan on the stove.

'Would you believe a variation on the theme of turkey?' she said with a laugh, and he chuckled.

'Smells good, whatever it is. Sort of Moroccan?'

'Mmm. A tagine. I found all the ingredients in the cupboard—I hope you don't mind?'

'Of course I don't mind. Use what you like. There doesn't look very much there, have you done enough for us all?'

'Oh. I'm feeding the children earlier. This is just for you.'

She caught his frown out of the corner of her eye. 'What about you?'

'I'll eat with the children—'

'Why?'

She turned and looked at him, not knowing what her role was any longer, not sure what he expected of her.

So she said so, and his brow pleated in a frown.

'I thought…I don't know. We seem to have all eaten together since Christmas Day. Breakfast, lunch, variation on a theme of turkey—I rather thought that was the way it was now.'

'But I'm supposed to be looking after you, helping you with the things you can't do, cooking for you—that's all.'

'Does that mean you can't eat with me?'

'Well…no, of course not, but I thought you might want to be alone—'

'No,' he said emphatically. 'Eat with me—please? Or, if there isn't enough, do something else—throw a bit more turkey in, or make a starter, but—no, I don't want to eat alone. And anyway, I thought we could talk about the job.'

The job. Of course. Nothing to do with wanting her company—and she shouldn't want him to, shouldn't be contemplating intimate little dinners *à deux*, or cosy drinks by the fire with the lights off and only the flickering flames to see by.

But that was what they ended up doing that evening, eating alone together after the children were in bed, opening a bottle of wine and then carrying the rest of it through to the drawing room, because they'd been in there during the day with Kate and Megan, doing a jigsaw by the fire while Thomas alternately slept or tried to haul himself up and eat the pieces.

Jake threw another log on, sat down at one end of the sofa at right angles to the fireplace and patted the seat beside him. 'Come and sit with me and talk,' he said. 'I've got some figures for you.'

And so she sat, hitching her feet up under her bottom and turning half towards him, studying him over her wine glass. 'Figures?'

He told her what he was prepared to pay, and she blinked. 'That's generous,' she said, and he shrugged.

'I expect a lot for my money.'

'And if I can't deliver?' she said with a shiver of dread. She hated to miss deadlines, hated letting people down, but— 'What if the children are sick, or Thomas won't sleep—what then?'

He shrugged. 'Then I expect you to let me know, to do the best you can and be upfront with me. Don't tell me you're doing it if you can't. Tell me if you've got a problem and I'll find another way round it. It's not impossible. We do it all the time. I'm not asking for an unbreakable commitment, just a promise to do your best to fulfil your side of the bargain. That's all any of us can ever do.'

'And if you don't think my work's up to scratch?'

'I know it will be. I know Barry Green. I've phoned him. He's gutted he had to let you down, but he's made some investments that have collapsed and it's not his fault. He really didn't have the money to pay you. In fact, he was relieved that I was going to be able to give you a job because he's been feeling really guilty. So—all I need to know is, will you take the job or do I need to look for someone else?'

Still she hesitated. So many reasons to take it—and so many not to.

'You don't have to deal with me, if that's what's troubling you,' he said softly. 'If you're worried about it all getting a bit too cosy, you can deal with Kate or my contracts manager. And it doesn't have to be for ever. If something better comes along, you can go. And Judith only wants a career break, she hasn't said she's stopping for ever—well, not yet. So it's only for the foreseeable future.'

He was making it so easy to say yes, so hard to say no. And the silly thing was, she didn't want to say no, but she was still afraid of getting involved. But she could deal with Kate, he said. That would be all right. Less complicated.

And so she nodded, her heart pounding as she said, 'Yes. OK. I'll take it. Thank you.'

He let out his breath on a soft huff of laughter. 'Good. Welcome to the team,' he said, lifting his glass and clinking it gently against hers, and she felt the smile spread over her face until it felt as if her whole body was glowing with relief.

'Thank you,' she said, and then as she lowered her glass, their eyes met and a breathless silence descended over them, broken only by the sharp crackling of the logs in the grate.

Oh, Lord. She could hardly breathe. Her eyes locked with his, the heat in them searing her to her soul. He reached out and took her glass and set it down beside his, and then his fingers curled around her jaw, his thumb grazing her bottom lip, dragging softly over the moist skin, the gentle tug bringing a whimper to her throat.

His fingertips traced her face, seeking out the fine lines around her eyes, the crease by her nose, the pulse pounding in the hollow of her throat.

'Come to bed with me,' he said softly, his voice gruff but gentle, and she felt her whole body responding to his touch, to his voice, to the need she could feel vibrating through his hand as it lay lightly against her collarbone.

'Is that wise?' she asked, with the last vestige of common sense, and gave a soft huff of laughter and he smiled.

'Probably not,' he said, but he stood up, holding out his hand to her and waiting, and after an endless pause she put her hand in his and let him draw her to her feet.

Her heart was pounding as he led her upstairs, his hand warm and firm around hers, his fingers sure. He closed the door with a soft click and pressed a switch, and the lights came on, soft and low, barely enough to see by.

'I'm not on the Pill,' she said, remembering in time another reason why this was a bad idea and why the last time it had been such a bad idea, too, but he shook his head.

'It's all right, I'll take care of it. Come here.'

And he drew her gently into his arms, folding her against his heart and just holding her for the longest time. Then she felt his warm breath against her neck, the soft touch of his hand easing the hair aside so he could press his lips to the skin, and she arched her neck, giving him access, desperate for the feel of his lips all over her body, the touch of his hand, the feel of his heart beating against hers.

She slid her hands under his cashmere sweater, so soft, and laid them against the heated satin of his skin. Hot skin, smooth, dry, taut over bones and muscles. She ran her palms up his spine, feeling the solid columns tense, the breath jerk in his lungs.

His hand cupped her jaw, tilting her head back, and his lips found hers, firm and yet yielding, his tongue coaxing her lips apart so that she opened for him with a tiny sound of need that brought an answering groan from low in his chest.

She could feel his hands at her waist, but her camisole was tucked into her jeans and his fingers plucked at it, a growl of frustration erupting from his lips. 'Too many clothes,' he muttered. 'I want to touch you, Amelia. I want to feel your skin against mine.'

Her legs buckled slightly and he caught her against him. 'I need you. This is crazy. Come to bed.'

And, moving away from her, he stripped off his clothes—the soft jumper, which was easy, then the jeans, harder, the stud exasperating him so that she took over and helped him, her knuckles brushing the taut, hard plane of his abdomen so that he sucked his breath in with a sharp hiss and seared her with his eyes.

They were like coals now, the slate-grey gone, banished by the inky-black of his flared pupils burning into her. The stud undone, he reached for her, peeling the sweater over her head, then the camisole, wrenching it out from her jeans with a grunt of satisfaction and then slowly sliding it up over her breasts, his eyes darkening still further as he let them linger on her.

And she'd never felt more wanted, had never felt more beautiful. He hadn't said a word, not a single compliment or facile remark, just the look in his eyes, which was turning her blood to rivers of fire.

He reached for her bra, giving her a moment of unease because after three children...but he unclipped it and eased it away, and his lids fluttered briefly before his eyes met hers. 'I need you,' he breathed.

'I need you, too. Jake, make love to me.'

'Oh, I intend to,' he said gruffly, then smiled a little off-kilter. 'Once you've undone the stud on your jeans.'

She laughed, releasing the tension that held her, and then he tugged them down once she'd undone the stud, and she stepped out of them and bent to pick them up, dragging another groan from his throat.

'That was my first view of you,' he said almost conversationally. 'When I walked into the breakfast room and you bent over to pick something off the table.' His hand stroked over her bottom, catching her hip with his fingertips and easing her back against his groin. She straightened up and saw their reflection in a mirror, his hand curled around her hip, his fingertips toying with the hem of her little lace shorts—the ones Kate had given her for Christmas.

Breathlessly she watched as his hand slid round, his fingers inside the edge tangling with the soft, damp curls and bringing a tiny gasp to her lips. He rocked against her, hard and solid and urgent, and she could see the tension in his face, the taut jaw, the parted lips, the dark, burning eyes.

His other arm was round her waist, the cast holding her firmly against him, the fingertips trailing over her skin.

And she couldn't play any more, she couldn't wait, couldn't hold on another moment. She needed him. She'd needed him all her life, and she didn't want to waste another second.

She turned in his arms, sliding her hands down inside his jeans and boxers, pushing them down just far enough, and he lifted her with one arm and carried her to the bed, dropping her on the edge and stripping away the scrap of lace before rummaging in the bedside table.

'Damn, can you help me? I can't do this with one hand,' he growled, and she took over, her fingers shaking as she touched him so intimately for the first time. His breath hissed in sharply, and then he paused, dragging in a ragged breath, his eyes closed, slowing his breathing until finally he opened his eyes and stared down at her body.

'Jake, please,' she breathed, and with a tortured sigh he went into her arms.

'Are you OK?'

She laughed softly. 'I don't know. I'll tell you in a minute,' she said, and he propped himself up on his elbow and stared down at her.

'You've got glitter in your hair,' she murmured, reaching up to touch it and testing the soft, silky strands between her fingers.

'Mmm. That would be your daughter,' he said, laughter in his voice. 'She thought it would be funny to sprinkle it on me—apparently it's fairy dust. It's going to make me rich.'

'Oh, well, that'll be handy,' she said with a chuckle.

He smiled at the irony. 'Do you have any idea how lovely you are?' he murmured, the fingertips of his left hand trailing slowly over her breasts. He brushed the knuckles over her nipple and it peaked for him obligingly, so he bent and took it in his mouth, suckling it hard and making her gasp.

'How is it I've fed three babies and yet that's so erotic?' she asked in wonder.

'I don't know. How about the other one?' he asked, bending over it. 'We ought to be fair and do a proper survey of both, just in case.'

'Idiot,' she said, but then his mouth closed over her and she forgot to speak, forgot her name almost—and forgot the reason why this was such a dangerous idea, such a silly thing to do as she gave herself up once more to the touch of his hands, the warmth of his lips, the solid, masculine body that could drive her to madness…

For the next week, while the office was still closed and the housekeeper was on her annual leave, they fell into a routine.

In the morning they had breakfast together, and then after they'd walked the dog and Thomas was back in his cot for his nap, Jake would go over to the office and she'd work on the laptop in the playroom upstairs while the children were amusing themselves, something they were very good at and which she encouraged.

And then Jake would come back and they'd have lunch,

and Thomas would nap again, and when he woke they'd have a swim while Jake worked again, and then she'd cook supper for all of them and after the children were in bed she'd fit in another couple of hours before he'd come and shut down her laptop, give her a glass of wine and then take her up to bed.

She didn't sleep with him, because of the children, but every night she went upstairs with him and he made love to her, slowly, tenderly, until her nerves were stretched to breaking point and she was pleading with him to end it.

But it couldn't go on like this, and they both knew it.

'I need to find a house,' she said, as they were standing in the attic on New Year's Eve watching the fireworks in the distance at midnight. 'New Year, new start. And now I've got a job, I can contact the agents and see what they've got—'

'You don't have to go,' he said quietly. 'You could stay—you and the children. Move in properly.'

'Live with you?'

'Yes.'

'No.' She shook her head. 'No, Jake, I can't,' she said, feeling the fear close in round her. 'I can't put us in anyone else's hands, ever again. I can't do that to myself, never mind my children. They've been through enough, and I can't ask it of them. I can't—' She broke off and shook her head again. 'I just can't. I'm sorry. Anyway, it's really sweet of you, but you don't mean it—'

'Sweet?' he said, his voice stunned. 'There's nothing sweet about it, Amelia. I want you. I need you. And I thought…hell, we were getting on so well.'

'We are—but that doesn't mean I can give up my independence, Jake—or theirs. I thought you understood that. I swore I'd never let another man have that much power over me.'

'How do I have power over you? You'd be sharing my life. I'd have no more power over you than you'd have over me.'

'But you would, because it's your house, and my only money is from you, and—it's called having all your eggs in one basket. Not a good idea.'

'It's OK if it's the right basket. Most of us do that, emotionally, at least, if not financially. Get another job if that's what's worrying you, although I have to say I'd be extremely reluctant to lose you. Don't walk away just because there's a chance it may not be right, because there's a much bigger chance, from where I'm standing, that it *is* right.'

'And how do I know? How do I know if it's right, Jake?'

He cradled her shoulders in his hands and met her eyes searchingly. 'You have faith,' he said softly. 'You have faith, and you give it your best shot, and if you're lucky, and you work at it, then all's well.'

'And if it's not? If we find out it's no good, that we aren't the people we thought we were?'

He sighed and dropped his hands. 'OK. It's too soon, I'm rushing you. But think about it. Don't dismiss it. Get somewhere else to live, and give us time. We can still see each other, have dinner, take the kids out—'

She shook her head. 'No. I don't want the kids coming to think of you as part of their life. This is different, we're staying here for a short time, you're doing us a favour. But if we move in properly, if it all gets too cosy and then it goes wrong—bang! Another rug out from under their feet. And I can't do it. I'm sorry.'

She felt tears clog her throat, and turned away. 'I'm sorry, Jake. It's been wonderful, but it ends when I leave. Or now. It's your choice.'

'Then come to bed with me,' he said, his voice rough with emotion. 'If I've only got you for a short while longer, I want to savour every moment.'

He thought it would tear him apart. Making love to her, knowing she was going, knowing he was losing her— It nearly broke him, but he needed to hold her, to love her, to show her without words just how infinitely sweet and precious she was to him.

He'd been a fool, imagining he could win her. She'd been so hurt, so damaged by her life with David and all its tortured twists and turns that it was no surprise she found it hard to trust. But he wouldn't give up. Somehow he'd find a way to convince her. He had to.

But then a week later, just before his housekeeper was due to return, she told him she'd found a house.

'Where?'

'About ten miles away—so I can still come in and see you if I need to for work.'

'Where is it?'

'In Reading.'

'Whereabouts?'

She sighed. 'Does it matter?'

He wanted to tear his hair out. 'Yes! Yes, it matters. What's it like? What's the area like?'

She wouldn't look at him, and that worried the hell out of him. 'Fine.'

He didn't believe her for a minute.

'Have you signed?'

'No. I'm going to see him tomorrow. I looked round it today.'

'And?'

She swallowed. 'It'll be perfectly all right.'

Damn it! He paced across the kitchen, then came back to her. 'I have an alternative—'

'I'm not living here, Jake!'

'Not here. Another house. You remember I said I lived somewhere else while this place was being done? It's empty. I was going to sell it, put it on the market in the spring. It's got four bedrooms, it's detached, the furniture's reasonable—it needs a clean, the tenant left yesterday, but it's close to Kate, it's in a good school catchment area, it's got a nice garden… Can you have pets in this house you've found?'

She sighed. 'I had to convince the letting agent he was all right. He's going to talk to the landlord.'

He stopped pacing and leant back against the worktop, his arms folded across his chest. 'And if he says no?'

She stared at him. 'Then I try again—Jake, why do you *care*?'

'Because I do,' he said honestly, and to hell with giving her time and not rushing her and letting her learn to trust him, because if she was going to go and live in some vile little house in a horrible area and send her kids to a grotty school, he was damned if he was going to stand back and let her do it. 'Because I love you, dammit!' And then his voice softened, his throat clogging. 'I love you, Amelia, and I can't make you stay here, but I can still keep you safe, and make you more secure. Take my rental house—I'll put it in your name, and you can have it. And you can work for me, or not. Your choice. But don't take your kids to some horrible area and put them in a ghastly school just—'

'Just what? Just what, Jake? Just because it's the best I can afford to do? Some of us don't have your options—'

'But I'm trying to *give* you options, and you're turning them down!'

'Because they're not options, Jake. They're just a honey trap—and I can't let you do this for us.'

'Then let me do it for the children. Let me put the house in their names, not yours. Let me give you the freedom to choose whether or not you want me, whether or not you can trust me enough to take my love at face value, and marry me. No strings, no ultimatums. The house is yours. The job is yours. And I'm yours—if you want me. Think about it. I'll get my solicitor on it in the morning. Let me have their full names.'

And he walked out of the room before he said anything else that might prejudice her against him, because he felt so close to losing her this time, and he didn't know what he'd do if he couldn't win her back.

CHAPTER TEN

'RIGHT, that's everything. Time to say goodbye. Say thank you to Jake.'

'I don't want to say goodbye,' Kitty wailed, wrapping her arms around his hips and hanging on for dear life.

'Nor do I,' Edward said, his chin wobbling, and Jake could understand that. His own chin was less than firm, and he had to clench his teeth to stop himself from saying something stupid, like, Stay.

'Jake, don't,' she said, and for a moment he thought he'd said it out loud, but she was just pre-empting him, her voice little more than a breath, and he nodded understanding.

No. Compliance. Not understanding. He couldn't understand for the life of him how she could tear herself away from him when it was going to leave him in tatters and he was pretty sure it would do the same for her, and for the children. But it was her choice, her decision, her life.

And she'd chosen to go. He peeled Kitty's arms away from his hips and lifted her up, hugging her gently and posting her into the car. 'Take care, sweetheart. Let me know how your new school is.'

She sniffed and nodded, and he kissed her wet little cheek and felt the lump in his throat grow larger. 'Take care, Tiger,' he said to Thomas, who just grinned at him, and then he ducked out of the car and turned and Edward was standing there. He dredged up a smile.

'Hey, sport. You'll be all right. Let me know about your voice test.'

'I don't want to go.'

'Yes, you do. Nothing might come of it anyway, but you might get a scholarship. You don't know unless you try. And you wouldn't have to be a boarder. Give it a go,' he encouraged, and then, because he could see Edward needed the reassurance, he held out his arms and hugged him.

'I want to stay here,' he mumbled into Jake's chest.

'I know, but you've got your own house now,' he told him, fighting down the emotion, making himself let go of a boy so like him it could have been him at the same age, with all the same emotional turmoil, the need to do the right thing. And that need was still with him, which was the only reason he could do what he did then, to let the boy go, to unwind his arms and push him gently towards the car and turn away.

To find Amelia there, standing awkwardly, twisting the keys in her hands and biting her lip. As he looked at her, her eyes welled with tears. 'Jake…I can't thank you…'

'Don't. Just go, if you have to. I can't do goodbyes.'

She nodded and got into the car, calling Rufus, but he refused to go. He sat down beside Jake and whined, and stupidly, that was the thing that brought tears to his eyes.

He blinked them savagely away, scooped the dog up and put him into the front footwell.

'Can I ring you?' Edward asked.

'Ask your mother. She's got my number. Take care, now—and good luck.'

He shut the door and stepped back, willing the engine to fail, but it started first turn and she drove away. He watched her until they reached the end of the drive and turned onto the road, and then he went back inside and shut the door.

It was so empty.

The house felt as if the very soul had been ripped out of it, and he wandered, lost, from room to room, the silence echoing with their laughter and tears, the squabbles of the children, the baby's gurgling laugh, the dog's sharp, excited bark, Amelia's warm, sexy chuckle, her teasing glances, the tenderness of her loving.

Gone, all of it, wiped out by her stubborn insistence on being independent.

And, hell, he could understand that. He'd grabbed his independence as soon as he could—as a child first at boarding school, then, with valuable life lessons learned, in senior school, and then in life itself, out there in the real world, cutting himself adrift from parents who'd never stopped bickering for long enough to understand him.

But he'd never walked away from love for fear of being hurt. If he had, he might never have married Rachel, never have known the joy of having a child, and for all it had been snatched away from him, he wouldn't have missed a second of it just because it hurt to lose it.

Better to have loved and lost...

But losing Amelia was so unnecessary! He wasn't *like* David. She didn't need to be cautious, because he wouldn't let them down, he wouldn't fail them with his lousy judgement or turn his back or walk away. He'd cut his own heart out before he'd hurt them, any of them. Even the damn dog.

He went into the sitting room, his sanctuary, and saw the recording of him singing. He'd never be able to listen to it again without thinking of Edward standing by the fire with the carol singers and filling the house with that sweet, pure sound.

He looked out of the window at the lump of slush on the lawn that was the remains of the snowman. The sprouts lay haphazard in the scarf, the carrot on the ground, and his hat had slid off sideways and was lying in a soggy heap.

They'd had such fun that day. They'd made snow angels as well, and eaten mountains of delicious food, and they'd played with their toys. Kitty had made him a picture with glitter, and then she'd sprinkled it in his hair.

Fairy dust.

And Amelia had found it that night, in bed, and teased him. The night he'd made love to her for the first time. He'd be finding glitter all over the house for months. Years, probably—

'Jake?'

There was a tap on the door, and it swung in and Kate stood there.

'Are you all right?'

'Why shouldn't I be?'

'I don't know. Why don't you tell me? You look like hell.'

'Thanks. What can I do for you?'

'I've got George Crosbie on the phone. I've been calling

your mobile and you haven't had it switched on. He's been trying to get you since yesterday.'

'Sorry. Switch it through to my study, I'll take it there. On second thoughts, I'll come over.'

Anything—even George—was better than sitting in the house on his own and listening to the echoes of the children.

He might have to stay over there all night.

'I hate it here.'

'It'll be lovely, Kitty, I promise. We'll soon make it nice. I'll get all our things out of store in the next few days, and we'll get settled in and it'll be home then.'

'Rufus isn't happy. He doesn't like it.'

He didn't. He sat by the front door and howled the whole time, as if he was hoping Jake would come. Amelia knew how he felt. She could have sat there and howled herself.

Edward was just quiet, retreating into himself as he'd done when David left. Not even the upcoming voice test in a week's time seemed to mean anything to him, and Millie didn't know what to do to help.

Apart from ring Jake and tell him it had all been a big mistake, but how could she? What if it all went wrong again? What if he got bored with the idea of another man's family? Your own was one thing, somebody else's was quite another. And David hadn't even wanted his own, so she didn't hold out hope for anyone else.

'Come on, it's time for bed.'

'I don't like my bed. It's lumpy.'

Hers wasn't. There wasn't a lump in it. Nothing so supportive. It was just saggy, saggy and uncomfortable and maybe even slightly damp. And there was a definite musty aroma that came off it, even through the sheets.

But she'd taken the house because the landlord hadn't demanded a huge deposit or dozens of references, he hadn't minded about the dog, and it was in budget. Just. She wanted to put by a good chunk of her money every month, just in case—

That was going to be carved on her headstone. 'Here lies Amelia Jones—Just In Case.'

'Come on, school tomorrow,' she said brightly. 'You need to get to bed.'

'I don't like the new school,' Edward said. 'I asked about a choir and they laughed.'

Oh, no. How much worse could it get?

'Heard anything from Amelia?'

'Yes. She says they're fine. She's done lots of work for you.'

'Yes. She's good.' Missing, but good. And how he missed her. Missed them all. 'Any news of Edward's voice test?'

She sighed and sat back on the sofa and met his eyes. 'Why don't you just ring them?'

'Because it's none of my business.'

She propped her elbows on her knees and planted her chin in her hands. 'You're in love with her, aren't you?'

'Do I pay you for this?'

'Yes. I'm your personal assistant—and, just now, I think you need a little personal assistance, so, yes, you do.'

He grunted. 'I could do with another coffee, if you want

to assist me,' he said bluntly, flicking open a file and scanning the contents.

'He doesn't want to go.'

'What?'

'Edward. He doesn't want to go to the voice test.'

Jake shut the file and stared at her searchingly. 'Why not?'

She shrugged. 'He wouldn't say, apparently. Just announced that he wasn't going, it was rubbish and he didn't want to sing any more, and that was it.'

'Well, maybe he doesn't,' he said slowly, although he didn't believe it for a moment. He'd been really fired up, keen to go, keen to find out all he could, and he'd been really excited when the invitation to attend the test had come through so quickly. So why—?

'I'm going to see her on Sunday. Any message?'

He slammed the door on temptation. 'No. She knows where to find me.'

'You give up easily.'

'No, I don't. But I'm not going to hound her. I gave her the choice, and she went. Her decision. I'm not going to beg.'

'I didn't ask you to beg, just not to give up—'

'Oh, for God's sake, Kate, I poured out my heart to her, told her things I've never told another soul! And she walked away. What else do you expect me to do?' he raged, jack-knifing to his feet and slamming his hand so hard against the window frame that the wood bit into the skin.

'Jake?' Kate's voice was tentative, her hand gentle on his shoulder. 'I'm sorry. I didn't mean to pry. But I can see you're unhappy, and...well, she is, too.'

He stared down the long walk, remembering the children running about having fun, throwing snowballs. 'There's nothing I can do about that. I haven't got the right or the power to do anything about that. Did she tell you I offered her the house in the village?'

'No. Could she afford it? I thought her rent budget was lower than that.'

'No—I mean, I offered to give it to her. Said I'd put it in her name. She said no, so I told her to give me the names of the children so I could put it in their names, and she refused. I thought—if she had a house, if she had independence—'

'But it wouldn't be, would it? It would be like being a concubine. Maybe you should have offered to marry her.'

He turned his head and met her eyes. 'I did. She said no.'

Kate's jaw dropped, and he pushed it up with his finger and smiled tiredly. 'Leave it now. I can't do this any more. I've told her I love her, I've asked her to marry me, I've offered her a house, I've given her a job—and the only thing she's taken is the job, which is her escape route from me. So I've taken the hint,' he said, his voice cracking. He cleared his throat. 'Right, I've done enough today, I'm going home. I'll see you on Monday.'

And he walked out of the office without a backward glance, went over to the house, shut the door of his sitting room, dropped into the sofa with a hefty glass of malt whisky and dedicated the next five hours to drowning his sorrows.

It didn't work.

* * *

'Jake looks awful.'

'Does he?'

'Yes—much like you. He told me he asked you to marry him and you said no. And he said you refused the house.'

'He talks too much,' she said tightly, closing the kitchen door so the children couldn't hear, and Kate laughed.

'I don't think so. Are you crazy? If a man like that asked me to marry him, I'd say yes like a shot.'

'What—because he's rich? It's meaningless.'

'No—because he's *nice*, Millie. He's a lovely guy. I can't understand why he's never been married before— although, come to think of it, he's never said that,' she went on thoughtfully. 'I wonder if he's divorced?'

'Don't ask me,' Amelia said, ignoring Kate's searching look, so Kate gave up and leant back against the worktop, her coffee cradled in her hands.

'He seemed shocked that Edward didn't want to do his voice test.'

Oh, *hell*. 'And how did he know that?'

'I told him.'

Millie sighed abruptly and stared at Kate in frustration. 'Do you and Jake do *nothing* at work except talk about me?'

'Oh, we fit in the odd bit—the occasional company takeover, a little asset-stripping, pruning out the dead wood, rolling the stock market dice—'

'Stop it! I don't want to hear it!'

Kate sighed. 'Millie, he's not like David. He doesn't do that. Yes, he buys companies, but he's considered, thoughtful, and he takes risks, sure, but only calculated ones—and here's the difference, he has a better calculator than David. He knows what he's doing, and he doesn't hurt innocent people along the way. If he did, I wouldn't work for him.'

No, she wouldn't, Amelia thought, staring down the bleak, scruffy little garden at the back of the house. Kate was too intrinsically decent to work for someone who wasn't. But that didn't mean that he was a safe bet personally. Maybe he was just lonely and thought they'd do to fill the gap in his life left by Rachel and Ben. Maybe he thought he could turn Edward into the son he'd lost, the son who could never grow up.

And her boy didn't deserve to be anybody's substitute. Even if that person was his hero—

'Give him another chance. At least see him. I'll babysit for you—you can tell the children you have to work, and they can come to me for a sleepover.'

Oh, she was so tempted. To see him again—it had only been a week, and she was missing him with every passing second. The rest of her life seemed like an eternity, stretching out in front of her without him.

A safe, dull, boring eternity.

'He hasn't contacted me. If he wanted to see me, he could ring.'

'You told him you didn't want him. Don't expect him to grovel. He said you know where to find him.'

So the ball was in her court.

Tough.

'I can't talk about this now. Not with the children here,' she said as their raised voices filtered through the door. 'Come on, we need to supervise this, it sounds a bit lively.'

Which made a change, because all week they'd been quiet and sad. Oh, damn.

'So—aren't you going to ask how they are?'

Oh, hell. He'd promised himself he wouldn't, but Kate would have known that, and she'd waited all day, keeping him in suspense, keeping him dangling.

'No,' he said bluntly. 'I'm not.'

'They're miserable. They were thrilled to see Megan, and Millie said it was the first time they'd laughed since they'd moved. And the dog sat by the door all day and whined.'

'Not my problem,' he said, his heart contracting into a tight ball in his chest. 'I've done all I can, Kate. I can't do more.'

But then later that week Kate came into his office looking worried.

'I've had a call from Millie. She can't finish that work you sent her—there's a problem.'

He leant back in his chair and looked up at her. 'What sort of a problem?'

'Rufus is ill. He's collapsed. She's taken him to the vet, but he's got to go to a referral centre. She's got Thomas with her and the children don't know—they need picking up from school. She's asked me if I can have Thomas and keep the children overnight—Jake, what are you doing?'

'Coming with you. She can't face this alone. I'll take my car and follow you.'

'What about your arm?'

'It's fine. She can drive from the vet's. Are you meeting her there?'

'Yes.'

'Right, let's go.'

He stuck his head into Reception on the way past. 'Clear my diary, and Kate's. We're going out,' he said, and followed Kate to the veterinary surgery.

She was standing by the door, pushing Thomas backwards and forwards in the stroller, trying to stop him crying while she watched the car park entrance for Kate's car.

'Come on, come on,' she muttered, and then she saw it turn in and her eyes flooded with tears of relief. 'Look, Thomas, it's Kate! You like Kate! You're going to stay with her—'

'How is he?'

She jerked upright. 'Jake?' she whispered, and then his arms were round her, and he was folding her against his heart and holding her tight.

'He's on a drip. They've sedated him—they think he might have had a stroke. They get them, apparently. I have to take him to a place miles away and I haven't got any petrol in the car—'

'I've got mine. You can drive it, I probably shouldn't with a cast on. Leave yours here, I'm sure they won't mind. Let's go and talk to them.'

'Where's Kate? I saw her car—'

'I'm here, sweetheart. I'll take Thomas. Give me your house keys. I'll pick up his stuff and some things for the others, and you can come and see me when you get back, OK?'

'OK,' she said, fumbling for her keys with nerveless fingers. 'Thank you.'

Her eyes flooded again, and Kate hugged her hard—difficult, because Jake still had one arm round her, holding her up—and then she was gone and Jake was steering her into Reception and talking to the staff.

Rufus was ready to go—the referral centre was expecting him—and she drove with one eye on the rear-view mirror, where she could see Jake sitting with Rufus beside him, still on the drip, the bag suspended above him clipped to the coat hook on the edge of the roof lining, his hand stroking the dog gently and murmuring soothingly to him.

He'd set the sat-nav to direct her, but although it took the stress out of finding the way, it left her nothing to worry about but Rufus. And the journey was interminable.

'Thank you so much for coming with me,' she said, what seemed like hours later as they sat outside waiting for news.

'Don't be silly,' he said, his voice gruff. 'I couldn't let you do this alone.'

'You always did like the stupid dog,' she said, her voice wobbling, and he put his arm round her shoulders and squeezed gently.

Not nearly as much as he liked the stupid owner, he thought, and then the door swung open and the vet who'd admitted Rufus came out to them.

'Mrs Jones?'

She leapt to her feet, but her legs nearly gave out and he held her up, his arm firmly round her waist, holding her tight as they waited for the news.

'We've done an MRI, and he has had a stroke,' the vet

said, and he felt a shudder go through her. 'It's in the back of his brain, the cerebellum, which controls balance. It's quite common in Cavaliers. Their skulls are a little on the small side and the vessels can get restricted, and he's got a little bleed, but we're going to keep him quiet and watch him, and hopefully it will heal and he'll recover. He's still very heavily sedated and we'll keep him like that for a while. The first few hours are obviously critical, and he's got through them so far, but until we can get this settled down and reduce the sedation we won't know if there's any lasting damage. I expect the unsteadiness he was showing will be worse, and he might stagger around in circles or hold his head on one side or just be unable to sort his feet out—it may be temporary, it may be permanent, or there may be a degree of permanent deficit, which is what I would expect. Do you have any questions?'

'Yes—how long will he be in?' she asked, her voice tight.

'Maybe a week. Possibly more.'

'Oh, no. Um…my insurance cover is only for three thousand pounds—'

'Don't worry about that,' Jake said firmly. 'Just do what you have to do and we'll sort it out later.'

She turned her face up to him, pale and shocked, the hideous, unpalatable decision clouding her lovely eyes. 'Jake, you can't do that—'

'Don't argue, Amelia,' he said firmly. 'Not about this. Will you keep in touch?' he added to the vet.

'I can't go—'

'There's nothing you can do here, Mrs Jones,' the vet said gently but firmly. 'Go home. We'll ring you if there's any change, and we'll ring you at seven in the morning and seven in the evening every day for an update.'

'Can I see him?'

'Of course. And you can come and visit him later in the week if he's progressing well, but we want him kept as quiet as possible for now.'

She nodded, and they were led through to see him. He was in a cage, flat on his side on a sheepskin blanket, with drips and oxygen and a heat lamp, and he looked tiny and vulnerable and very, very sick.

Jake felt his eyes prickle, and beside him Amelia was shaking like a jelly.

'Come on, I'm taking you home,' he said firmly, and led her out to the car park. He drove—he probably shouldn't have, with the cast on, but she certainly wasn't fit to drive, so he buckled her in beside him and set off. He could see her knotted hands working in her lap out of the corner of his eye, and her head was bent; he thought she was probably crying.

She lifted her head as they crunched onto the gravel drive, and looked around. 'Why are we here?'

'Because Kate's got your house keys, and I think you need a little TLC in private for a while,' he said, and cut the engine. 'Come on.'

He led her inside, and as soon as the door closed behind them, she collapsed against his chest, sobbing.

'I can't lose him,' she wept. 'I can't—how can I tell the children? I can't take him away from them as well—'

'Shh. Come and sit down, I'll get you a drink.'

'I don't want a drink, I want Rufus,' she said, abandoning all attempt at courage, and he steered her into his sitting room, pushed her down onto the sofa and dragged her into his arms.

She cried for ages, not only for the dog, he suspected, but for all the things she'd lost, the things that had gone wrong, the agonies and disappointments and bitter regrets of the past several years.

And then finally she hiccupped to a halt, her eyes puffy and red-rimmed, her cheeks streaked with drying tears, her mouth swollen. And he'd never seen anything more beautiful in his entire life.

'Better now?'

She nodded, sniffing again, and he hugged her and stood up. 'Come on, let's get something to eat and tell Kate what's happening,' he said gently, and she let him pull her up and lead her through to the kitchen.

There was a note on the island from his housekeeper.

CASSEROLE IN FRIDGE. TOP OVEN, HALF AN HOUR. VEG IN MICROWAVE. FIVE MINUTES.

'Hungry?' he asked. She shook her head, but he didn't believe her, so he put the casserole in the top oven anyway and put the kettle on, then rang Kate.

'Hi. He's doing all right, but the next few hours are critical, so I've got her at home. I don't want her by herself. Can you keep the kids?'

'Of course. I won't be in tomorrow, then.'

'No, I know. Nor will I. I'll keep in touch. Thanks, Kate. I think Amelia wants to talk to you.'

He handed the phone over and listened as she tried hard to be brave and upbeat—talking to the children, he guessed, because she said the same thing three times—to Kate, then to Kitty, then to Edward—and then she turned to him. 'Edward wants to talk to you.'

Oh, hell. He took the phone out of her hand. 'Hi, Edward. How are things?'

'Horrible. Is Rufus really going to be OK?'

'I hope so,' he said, refusing to lie to the child. 'They're very skilled, and if he can get through this, he'll do it there, but we're all thinking about him, and if thinking can help, then he'll make it for sure.'

'Thinking doesn't help,' he said. 'I keep thinking about living with you, but it hasn't helped at all.'

'We can't always have what we want,' he said gently. 'You have to change the things you can, and find the strength to deal with the things you can't. Like this voice test. Kate said you didn't want to go.'

'But what's the point? We can't afford it—and anyway, if Rufus dies, I can't leave Mummy, can I?'

'OK. One thing at a time. You have to be offered a place first, and see if you'd like to do it. Then you worry about paying. There might be a way—a scholarship, for instance. That was how I got there. My parents didn't have any money, and the choir school paid my fees. And Rufus hasn't died, and there's every chance he'll live and get better, although it may take a while. And you could probably go to the school as a day boy, so you wouldn't have to leave your mother.'

There was a silence at the end of the line.

'Edward?' he prompted.

'Mmm.'

'Don't shut doors until you know what's on the other

side. It might be what you're looking for, it might not. But you owe it yourself to find that out. Do you want to talk to your mum again?'

'No, it's OK. Tell her I love her.'

'OK. We'll be in touch. Don't worry. He's in the best place.'

He turned off the phone and set it down. 'I have to give you a message,' he said, turning towards her. 'I love you.'

She looked up into his eyes, startled. 'What did you say?'

'I love you.'

Something—hope?—flared in her eyes, and then died. 'That's the message?'

'Yes. So does Edward. That's his message.'

He saw the hope dawn again, then saw her fight it, not allowing herself the luxury of his love, because she didn't dare to trust him—and there was nothing more he could do to prove to her that he loved her, that she and her family and her dog had a home with him, a place in his heart for ever.

He stepped back. 'I'll make the tea,' he said gruffly, and turned away, the pain of knowing he would never have her in his life too great to stand there in front of her and make civilised conversation about her son and her dog and—

'Jake?'

He paused and put the kettle down. 'What?'

'I'm sorry. I've been so stupid. I've kept thinking you were like David, that under it all you were the same kind of person, pursuing the same goals, but you're not, are you? You're just in the same line of business. He always wanted to get rich quick, but you've got where you are by doing what you can to the best of your ability, by working hard, paying attention to detail, doing it right. And you've been successful, not lucky, because you're good at what you do and you do what you're good at.

'And you're good at being a father, Jake. You've been more of a father to my children in the last few weeks than their own father ever has, and a better man to me than he could ever be. And, as for Rufus—there's no *way* David would have done everything you've done for him. He would have told the vet to put him down, because he didn't realise how important he was to the children, how much he's given them. Not that he would have cared. He never gave them anything without considering it first, but you—when your heart was breaking, you gave us Christmas, even though it must have hurt you unbearably, because it was the right thing to do. And you do that, don't you? The right thing. Always.

'So, if the offer's still open—if you really meant it, if you really do love me and want to marry me—then nothing would make me prouder than to be your wife—'

She broke off, her voice cracking, and he turned slowly and stared at her. Her eyes were downcast, her lip caught between her teeth, and he reached out gently and lifted her chin.

'Was that a yes?' he asked softly, hardly daring to breathe, and she laughed, her eyes flooding with tears.

'Yes, it was a yes,' she said unsteadily. 'If you'll still have me—'

'Stuff the tea,' he said. 'I've got a better idea.'

And, scooping her up in his arms, he carried her upstairs to bed.

* * *

'What's that smell?'

'The casserole. Damn.'

He got up and walked, still naked, out of the bedroom and down to the kitchen. She pulled on his shirt and followed him, arriving in the kitchen as he set the casserole dish down on the island. 'Oops.'

'Oops, indeed. Never mind. We'll grab something on the way to Kate's.'

'Kate's?'

'Mmm. I think we need to tell the children—and then we've got wedding plans to make. How do you fancy a January wedding?'

She blinked. 'Two weeks, max? That's tight.'

'Why? We've got the venue. We'll get married in the church, and we'll come back here and celebrate. It's not like it's going to be a huge affair. Your family, our friends—twenty or so? The people from work are my family, really—so more than twenty. OK. It's getting bigger,' he admitted with a laugh, and she hugged him.

'And two weeks isn't long enough to be legal. I don't care when I marry you, or where, just so long as I can be with you.'

It was May, in the end.

Her brother-in-law gave her away—Andy, who'd apologised for the way he and Laura had treated her at Christmas. He had finally told her that they were unable to have children, which was why they'd found it so hard to have the children there. Kate was her matron of honour with Kitty and a slightly wobbly Rufus in a brand-new collar as her attendants.

And Edward, who'd been practising for weeks with the choir master at his new school, sang an anthem which reduced them both to tears, and then after the service they walked back to the walled garden where the fountain was playing, and in a pause in the proceedings Jake turned to her and smiled.

'All right, my darling?'

'Much better than all right. Have I ever told you that I love you?'

He laughed softly. 'Only a few thousand times, but it took you long enough, so I'm quite happy to hear it again.'

'Good,' she said, squeezing his arm, 'because I intend to keep telling you for the rest of my life...'

Bestselling author Lynne Graham is back with a fabulous new trilogy!

PREGNANT BRIDES

Three ordinary girls—naive, but also honest and plucky...
Three fabulously wealthy, impossibly handsome and very ruthless men...
When opposites attract and passion leads to pregnancy... it can only mean marriage!

Available next month from Harlequin Presents®: the first installment

DESERT PRINCE, BRIDE OF INNOCENCE

* * *

'THIS EVENING I'm flying to New York for two weeks,' Jasim imparted with a casualness that made her heart sink like a stone. 'That's why I had you brought here. I own this apartment and you'll be comfortable here while I'm abroad.'

'I can afford my own accommodation although I may not need it for long. I'll have another job by the time you get back—'

Jasim released a slightly harsh laugh. 'There's no need for you to look for another position. How would I ever see you? Don't you understand what I'm offering you?'

Elinor stood very still. 'No, I must be incredibly thick because I haven't quite worked out yet what you're offering me....'

His charismatic smile slashed his lean dark visage. 'Naturally, I want to take care of you....'

HPEX0110A

'No, thanks.' Elinor forced a smile and mentally willed him not to demean her with some sordid proposition. 'The only man who will ever take *care* of me with my agreement will be my husband. I'm willing to wait for you to come back but I'm not willing to be kept by you. I'm a very independent woman and what I give, I give freely.'

Jasim frowned. 'You make it all sound so serious.'

'What happened between us last night left pure chaos in its wake. Right now, I don't know whether I'm on my head or my heels. I'll stay for a while because I have nowhere else to go in the short term. So maybe it's good that you'll be away for a while.'

Jasim pulled out his wallet to extract a card. 'My private number,' he told her, presenting her with it as though it was a precious gift, which indeed it was. Many women would have done just about anything to gain access to that direct hotline to him, but his staff guarded his privacy with scrupulous care.

Before he could close the wallet, his blood ran cold in his veins. How could he have made such a serious oversight? What if he had got her pregnant? He knew that an unplanned pregnancy would engulf his life like an avalanche, crush his freedom and suffocate him. He barely stilled a shudder at the threat of such an outcome and thought how ironic it was that what his older brother had longed and prayed for to secure the line to the throne should strike Jasim as an absolute disaster....

* * *

What will proud Prince Jasim do if Elinor is expecting his royal baby? Perhaps an arranged marriage is the only solution! But will Elinor agree? Find out in DESERT PRINCE, BRIDE OF INNOCENCE by Lynne Graham [#2884], available from Harlequin Presents® in January 2010.

REQUEST YOUR FREE BOOKS!
2 FREE NOVELS PLUS 2
FREE GIFTS!

HARLEQUIN *Romance*

From the Heart, For the Heart

YES! Please send me 2 FREE Harlequin® Romance novels and my 2 FREE gifts (gifts are worth about $10). After receiving them, if I don't wish to receive any more books, I can return the shipping statement marked "cancel." If I don't cancel, I will receive 4 brand-new novels every month and be billed just $3.84 per book in the U.S. or $4.24 per book in Canada. That's a savings of at least 15% off the cover price! It's quite a bargain! Shipping and handling is just 50¢ per book.* I understand that accepting the 2 free books and gifts places me under no obligation to buy anything. I can always return a shipment and cancel at any time. Even if I never buy another book, the two free books and gifts are mine to keep forever.

114 HDN EYU3   314 HDN EYKG

Name	(PLEASE PRINT)	
Address		Apt. #
City	State/Prov.	Zip/Postal Code

Signature (if under 18, a parent or guardian must sign)

Mail to the **Harlequin Reader Service:**
IN U.S.A.: P.O. Box 1867, Buffalo, NY 14240-1867
IN CANADA: P.O. Box 609, Fort Erie, Ontario L2A 5X3

Not valid to current subscribers of Harlequin Romance books.

**Are you a subscriber of Harlequin Romance books
and want to receive the larger-print edition?
Call 1-800-873-8635 today!**

* Terms and prices subject to change without notice. Prices do not include applicable taxes. Sales tax applicable in N.Y. Canadian residents will be charged applicable provincial taxes and GST. Offer not valid in Quebec. This offer is limited to one order per household. All orders subject to approval. Credit or debit balances in a customer's account(s) may be offset by any other outstanding balance owed by or to the customer. Please allow 4 to 6 weeks for delivery. Offer available while quantities last.

Your Privacy: Harlequin Books is committed to protecting your privacy. Our Privacy Policy is available online at www.eHarlequin.com or upon request from the Reader Service. From time to time we make our lists of customers available to reputable third parties who may have a product or service of interest to you. If you would prefer we not share your name and address, please check here. ☐

HR09R

HARLEQUIN® Romance®

ESCAPE AROUND *the* WORLD

Dream destinations, whirlwind weddings!

The Daredevil Tycoon

by

BARBARA MCMAHON

A hot-air balloon race with Amalia Catalon's sexy daredevil boss, Rafael Sandoval, is only the beginning of her exciting Spanish adventure....

Available in January 2010 wherever books are sold.

HARLEQUIN *Romance*

Coming Next Month

Available January 12, 2010

Fall in love in 2010—with Harlequin® Romance!

#4141 THE ITALIAN'S FORGOTTEN BABY Raye Morgan
Baby on Board
Marco has lost two weeks of his life and wants them back. After an accident on holiday left him with amnesia, he's returned to the beautiful island to find his memories—and a baby bombshell!

#4142 THE DAREDEVIL TYCOON Barbara McMahon
Escape Around the World
A hot-air balloon race with her daredevil boss, Rafael, is only the beginning of Amalia's Spanish adventure....

#4143 JUST MARRIED! Cara Colter and Shirley Jump
You're invited to two very special weddings! Grab a glass of champagne for bridesmaid Samantha's big day and a handful of confetti for when best man Colton ties the knot!

#4144 THE GIRL FROM HONEYSUCKLE FARM Jessica Steele
In Her Shoes...
Phinn isn't fooled by eligible bachelor Ty's good looks, and sparks fly when she discovers he's the hotshot London financier who bought her beloved Honeysuckle Farm.

#4145 ONE DANCE WITH THE COWBOY Donna Alward
Cowboy Drew left Larch Valley promising Jen he'd return. When he didn't, she moved on.... Now Drew's back! Could *Cowboys and Confetti* be on the horizon? Find out in the first of a brand-new duet.

#4146 HIRED: SASSY ASSISTANT Nina Harrington
9 to 5
Medic Kyle has swapped the wilds of Nepal for Lulu's English country house. He wants to publish her famous mother's diaries—that is if he can get this sassy assistant to play ball.